STRAY CAT

SHIFTERS UNBOUND
BOOK 16

JENNIFER ASHLEY

JA / AG PUBLISHING

CHAPTER ONE

G *ravity is a state of mind ...*
Lindsay repeated this as she clung with cat claws to the overhead beam, her muscles straining to prevent herself from plunging thirty feet to the hard arena floor.

Xavier Escobar was down there, in a pool of electric lantern light, talking to some very bad guys. He was alone for now, counting on his powers of persuasion to keep the men he negotiated with from shooting him dead.

Xav had no idea that Lindsay, in her lynx form, lurked above, ready to assist. That is, if the fall didn't kill her.

Shifter Felines are badass. She drummed the words through her head. *Indestructible.* Besides, gravity was only a theory.

Or was it a law? Or were there laws of gravity, and gravity itself was a theory? She should have paid more attention in science class.

"Look, asshole, I just want the money," Xavier said below her.

Xav was playing a minor tough. His mission: Infiltrate an impenetrable gang who'd in the past murdered two under-cover cops.

Because the gang leaders had detailed information on all Las Vegas police detectives, the LVMPD had hired Xav and his brother Diego to help them out. While Diego and Xav had been with the police department in the past, the gang had become active in the area only after Xav and Diego had quit the force to open their own private security agency.

Xav still had many friends in the LVMPD, and he hadn't been able to turn away their call for assistance.

"Watch your mouth," the leader of the group said to Xav. "You'll get paid. But I need to know who your contact is before I decide if I can trust you."

Xav heaved an exaggerated sigh. "I don't like to give up my friends."

"You're not giving them up. I'm trying to make sure you're not a cop, a spy, or someone horning in on my territory."

Xav nodded. "I get it. You don't know me, so why should you hand me a bag of money? Even though I brought you good pieces."

He nudged the wooden box at his feet, which contained several long-barreled guns. Lindsay wasn't certain what kind they were, because she had no interest in weapons. That was a human thing.

"Exactly," the leader said. "If you stole these from another gang, I don't want them coming after us. They wouldn't last long, but it would be a hassle. Then the police might decide to investigate, and that's even more hassle. Save me a lot of time if you just told me where you got them."

Xav lifted his hands in a conceding gesture. "Okay, okay."

Xav had dressed the part in old jeans, black T-shirt, and a hoodie that covered his nearly black hair. He hadn't shaved, and a beard shadow darkened his face. Xav liked to be neat and clean, so this was a different look for him.

Lindsay longed to tell him how sexy he was, but she

couldn't while she crouched precariously thirty feet up, her paws starting to ache.

"So, come on," the tough said. "Who is he?"

Xav flashed the man a grin. "Not he. She. Emma Shields."

Lindsay couldn't see the expression on the man's face from this height, but the change in his scent said he was impressed.

"Shields? She trusts you?"

"Obviously." Xav shrugged. "She knows what she's doing, so they'll be good."

Lindsay fought a sudden dart of jealousy. He'd gone to see Emma, had he?

Emma Shields was a former member of the underworld who now worked off and on for Xav and Diego. She had a reputation for being fair and straightforward, as long as you didn't piss her off. Most of the criminal gangs hadn't realized she'd started working against them, and they more or less still trusted her.

Xav considered Emma personable and smart, and he talked about her a lot. Emma was also human, so no problems with Xav taking her out to places Shifters weren't welcome, or with her becoming a snarling cat whenever she had PMS.

Lindsay tamped down her anger with effort. Xav and Lindsay didn't have a relationship in the strictest sense, or a *thing*, or sometimes even friendship. They hung out when they got along and avoided each other when one of them was in a snit, which was mostly Lindsay. Xav rarely got mad about anything.

Even now, Xav remained calm and collected. He might pretend to be agitated about dealing with such a prominent and dangerous gang member, but Lindsay knew that on the inside, Xav was as cool as the winter wind.

Which, by the way, was blowing like mad outside the deserted arena. The roof rattled in an alarming manner.

It grew so loud Lindsay almost missed what happened next on the floor. A large guy stepped to the man speaking to Xav and whispered something into his ear.

Lindsay sensed an immediate change in the leader's body language, stance, and scent. "Deal's changed, dude," he snapped at Xav.

"What?" Xav asked in bewilderment. "Why? You don't like Emma?"

"We like her fine. But we don't like *you*. You hang out with Shifters, don't you?"

"What are you talking about?" Xav continued in genuine surprise. But he didn't slip from his persona, and Lindsay sensed him decide not to lie. He went with it. "Anyway, so what? They're cool. I might have a beer with one, once in a while."

"Who says you didn't bring some with you tonight?" the leader persisted. "Who says that when we walk out of here, a pack of them won't jump us and take these pieces back for you?"

Xav managed a scornful laugh. "Because Shifters don't like firearms, man. They don't use them. They don't need them."

Damn right. Claws, teeth, and lightning-swift reflexes outdid human weapons any day. Shifters were good at surviving gunshots as well.

Humans weren't, though. The black pistol the leader pulled on Xav made Lindsay's heartbeat hammer off the scale.

She stared at the guy's head, calculating the twist and angle she'd have to make to land on him without smashing herself to the ground. Now was the time to test the legend that cats always landed on their feet.

Xav continued talking. He had a smooth voice and could persuade anyone to do anything he wanted. He could convince Lindsay to do whatever as well, she thought with a dark shiver, but she never let on.

"Now, come on," Xav was saying. "These pieces are legit. I mean, they'll never be traced. Not to you, not to me. Emma's good. You know that."

"She is, yeah. You, I'm not so sure about. Tell you what. Leave the box. I'll check it out with Emma and give *her* the money. Then she can pay you."

"What?" Xav took a step back, glaring in outrage. "I thought we were doing a deal. I'm not standing out here in this freezing arena for my health. I need the money, man. Come on."

He was stalling, Lindsay realized. Diego and whatever police would be listening in, no doubt through the wireless tech that DX Security specialized in. Xav must be waiting for them to catch up, or maybe he was trying to indicate exactly where inside the arena he stood.

Xav needed to make the gang leader believe he was nothing more than what he appeared to be—a small-time dealer who'd seen an opportunity to make a few bucks. His air of desperation hinted that he owed even badder people money and couldn't afford to walk away from this transaction.

"Not a negotiation, my friend," the leader said. "Leave it. Get out."

"Shit." Xav made every show of frustration mixed with resignation. "Emma told me you were cool. Well, you get to answer to *her* now. All because I know a few Shifters?"

"More than know them. You're screwing one, I heard."

"Huh?" Xav's puzzlement was unfeigned, but Lindsay's danger signals went off all over the place.

Had the guy seen her and Xav together? But then, Xav

wouldn't have been in his current disguise when he was with Lindsay. He'd have worn his usual tight-fitting button-downs, or Henleys and jeans, or maybe a subdued, dark suit. He looked so good in those ...

How did these guys know Xav had Shifter friends and a Shifter sort-of girlfriend? Xav went to Shiftertown all the time, because Diego, mated to Lindsay's best friend, lived there now.

If someone knew Xav was Diego's brother and had reported it to the leader, that meant Xav's cover was blown.

Shit, shit, shit.

Where was Diego? Or a barrage of cops ready to kick through the doors and throw the gang members to the ground?

"Turn around." The lead man's tone said he was done with the discussion. "Walk away. Or I shoot you. I don't miss. Either way, I'm leaving with the box. You can decide whether you leave with your life."

"Okay." Xav drew out the word in shaky irritation. "Damn, I just needed some cash."

Xav turned around slowly. He let his shoulders droop in perfect imitation of a guy who knew he'd lost and could only curse and kick at the dust on his way out.

The leader brought up his pistol and aimed it directly between Xav's shoulders.

Lindsay screamed. Because she was in wildcat form, it came out a growling screech as she launched herself downward at the man with the gun.

She landed right on him. At her yowl, the leader and his friends scanned the dark arena in startled confusion but never pinpointed Lindsay until she was on the man's head, claws sinking deep into his flesh.

His gun went off, again and again, but the man's aim was

wild, bullets pinging against steel rafters. His guys and Xav hit the dirt.

Lindsay lunged down the man's arm and wrapped her mouth around his wrist. One chomp, and the pistol clattered to the floor, blood streaming after it.

The leader screamed and cursed, spinning in place as he tried to pry Lindsay off him, but Lindsay had dug in and wasn't letting go.

Xav, on his feet again, busily relieved the other three gang members of weapons they'd drawn to shoot at Lindsay. Lindsay couldn't see exactly what Xav did, but there were many kicks and punches, swearing and shouts.

Diego and several other guys in black fatigues and police uniforms joined the fray. The arms dealers were on the ground, cuffs clicking into place.

The leader continued to struggle against Lindsay, pleading for someone to get this fucking cat off him.

Hands landed on Lindsay's back. Her fur was thick, but she instantly recognized Xav's touch.

"Let him go, Linds."

Xav's rumbling voice, even tinged with anger, sparked rippling heat deep inside Lindsay. Maybe she'd let Xav pry her off the scumbag. He'd cuddle her against him, trying to calm her down. Though Shifter lynxes were twice the size of wild ones, Lindsay was still small enough to lie against Xav while he stroked her ...

"*Now,*" Xav commanded.

Damn it. Lindsay opened her mouth, releasing the guy's wrist. She'd barely broken the skin—the supposedly dangerous gang leader was such a baby.

She peeled her large claws from the man's arm and shoulder, one talon at a time. Lynxes had lots of fur on their paws to cushion them against snow, ice, and thorny brush, so the man's hard arms hadn't hurt her one bit.

Plus, her aim had been spectacular. Had Xav noticed that?

Lindsay unhooked the last of her claws and bounded to the ground. She sat down on her haunches next to Xav and calmly started washing her face.

Diego cuffed the leader's wrists behind him, a look of satisfaction on his face.

"This is why I hate Shifters," the leader declared. He spat at Lindsay.

Lindsay easily evaded him and returned to Xav's side, watching complacently as Diego and the other DX Security men led the bad guys away. She made sure her ear tufts stood straight up, indicating she was focused on the leader, watching him. Also, they were cute.

Xav threw back the hood of his jacket, revealing rumpled dark hair Lindsay loved to run her hands through when they danced. Even more whenever they kissed.

His eyes were dark like a moonless night, liquid and warm, but right now, they were filled with incandescent fury.

"Want to tell me what the hell you're doing here?" Xav demanded. "And why you thought it was a great idea to interrupt a multi-month sting? There are a dozen cops outside who will arrest you in a heartbeat if that loser complains about you. What the fuck were you thinking?"

CHAPTER TWO

I was thinking I just saved your life, Lindsay growled.

She couldn't answer in a way Xav would understand while she was still a lynx, so she gave him an angry cat stare before she stomped off to the backpack she'd left hidden under the first row of bleacher seats.

Fortunately, Xav gave her some privacy to go through the annoying contortions it took to morph back into her human form. Some Shifters could flow easily into their animal and back again, but Lindsay's shift required time and energy.

Once she rose on human legs, which were sore from hanging onto the rafters, she pulled clothes out of her backpack. On went undies, jeans, and a thin T-shirt, leaving off the heavier shirt and jacket she'd worn earlier. It was cold outside, but Lindsay was always hot after shifting.

Xav didn't look any less angry by the time Lindsay returned to him. The fact that he'd waited for her gave her hope—he could have stormed off and left her on her own.

They'd settle this and then go out, she decided. Xav would cool down, and they'd have a night of fun.

Xav apparently wasn't interested in fun. "Those guys

meant business, Linds. They'd have shot you dead without a second thought if they'd known you were here. Where were you, anyway?"

Lindsay pointed upward. Xav tilted his head back to gaze at the truss that held up the roof. The beams were barely visible to Lindsay in the dim light, which meant Xav's human vision wouldn't see them at all. But he knew what they looked like—every spring Xav brought an at-risk boy's group out here to coach them in basketball.

"Seriously?" Xav switched his glare back to Lindsay. "I know you think you're an indestructible Shifter, but you could have died from that jump."

Lindsay realized her choices had been less than good tonight, but it wasn't in her nature to hang her head and take a scolding.

She planted one hand on her hip. "Yeah, but did you see me stick that landing? It was awesome."

And a great relief. She'd proved she *could* jump thirty feet, hit her target, and survive. Cats really did land on their feet. Or on someone else's head.

Xav's expression didn't soften. "I know you wanted to help. You were worried, and I appreciate that. But I had Diego and our guys a step away, not to mention all those cops, and we were following a plan. We had it covered."

Lindsay lost her feigned nonchalance. "Humans can't move as fast as Shifters," she said heatedly. "That man was going to shoot you, Xav, right between your shoulder blades. You'd have died. I wasn't going to let that happen." She matched his scowl with a fearsome one of her own. "You're welcome."

"I'm wearing a vest, Linds." Xav pulled up an inch of his shirt to show her padded black fabric. DX Security's bullet-proof vests were less bulky than what most cops wore, thanks to Xav's connections to people who made state-of-the-art defensive tech. "I knew he'd try to shoot me at some point. Figures he'd wait until my back was turned."

"You'd still have been on the ground, and maybe out of it for a few days. And what if Diego hadn't come in fast enough? The guy could have shot you in the head—or is that a Kevlar hoodie?" She pointed at the jersey fleece that hung down his back.

"A lot of things could have happened." Xavier's growl told her he'd reached the end of his patience. "If you'd missed him, if he'd shot you instead ..."

Xav caught Lindsay by the wrists. She hoped he'd pull her into an embrace, lower her head to his shoulder, and confess how much he'd hate it if she were hurt.

Xav let out a breath without doing any of those things. "I don't want to explain to your parents—or to Cassidy—why I let you get yourself killed. Cassidy would drag me up to those rafters and dangle me off them, and you know it. I understand you had good intentions, but you have to let me handle these jobs the way we plan them."

Lindsay jerked from his grip. "You *needed* me here, Xav. Humans are unpredictable, but I can scent what they're going to do before they do it. I had to follow you and hide because you refused to tell me what you were up to tonight. I didn't know what to think. Maybe you had another lady stashed away." Lindsay pretended to ease back on her indignation and move to flirtation. "I didn't want to be jealous."

Something warm flashed in Xav's eyes, and for a moment, Lindsay thought he'd relent. He'd tug her to him, tell her he couldn't stay mad at her, and they'd go dancing. Xav liked to dance, and he was good at it.

Xav's hardness returned. "If our detainee complains that a Shifter attacked him, the case against him can be thrown out. A Shifter assault is considered more egregious in the eyes of the law than a gun deal gone bad. Also, he might mention that your Collar didn't go off. How are you going to explain that?"

Lindsay listened in disquiet. She knew Xav was right—the stupid laws and rules about Shifters put her status beneath that of a lowlife peddling weapons to even worse people.

Her Collar hadn't gone off, because it was a fake. When Shifters had first been exposed to the rest of the world, Shifter Bureau had fitted them with Collars that were part tech, part Fae magic that fired excruciating shocks whenever a Shifter grew violent.

A while back, Eric and another Shiftertown leader had figured out how to remove the Collars and create fakes. Lindsay and her family had already had theirs replaced, so Lindsay could rescue Xav tonight without pain to herself. However, If any human figured out that the Collars no longer worked, all Shifters could be endangered.

Xav was correct that Lindsay hadn't thought about whether her impulsive actions would curtail Xav or cause more problems than they solved. She'd only wanted to keep him safe from people who wouldn't hesitate to leave his dead body here for the cleaners to find.

She'd pictured him being grateful, maybe celebrating with her when they went back to Shiftertown. He might invite her to his new place, where they could celebrate in private.

That clearly was not going to happen tonight. Lindsay had only succeeded in making Xav mad at her for everything that *could* have happened. And yeah, if the guy claimed a Shifter assaulted him, the whole operation would be for nothing.

Lindsay stepped back, so Xav wouldn't see she was about to do something stupid and cry. She had to maintain the seductive bearing she always took with Xav, teasing him and tempting him, so she'd maintain some sort of influence in their relationship.

Their *non*-relationship, she corrected herself. There'd been no commitments, no exclusivity. Only the two of them getting together when they felt like it, neither of them admitting to wanting more than that.

Lindsay wanted a *lot* more. But tonight, she'd blown it.

"Convince the police that the Shifter attack had nothing to do with DX Security," she said in a steady voice. "Which would be easier if you hadn't called me by name. But you can do it. Everyone listens to you." Lindsay considered all the other things she could add to her argument—rebuking him for not being more careful, pointing out that he could have explained to her about the mission first place.

She decided it was time for an exit.

"See ya, Xav."

Lindsay turned her back on him, standing straighter and more confidently than she felt at the moment. She scooped up her bag and walked away, letting her hips swing.

Xav said absolutely nothing as Lindsay made her way to the nearest door. She resisted looking back as she went, not wanting to spoil her departure.

When she reached the outer hall that ran all the way around the arena, she couldn't stop herself peeking back in through the open doorway.

Xav was gone. He'd probably tramped away the minute she'd sashayed off and hadn't witnessed her attempt to make him regret her leaving.

Damn it.

Lindsay pushed through an outer door to the parking lot and let it slam behind her. This side of the arena was deserted—Diego and the cops were around the other side with their catch for the night.

She quickly made for her tiny blue car, parked in the

darkness beyond any lights. She'd left a minute dress and her party shoes in the back seat, in anticipation of this evening ending differently.

Once inside her car, Lindsay started it up and got the hell out of there. She ignored the vans hunkering beyond the arena, and the seriously sexy human man who was talking quietly with his brother.

Though she longed to peel out and roar away in a cloud of dust, Lindsay knew that would be a stupid move. She drove quietly away from the arena, heading into Las Vegas and making for her favorite dance club, the ache in her heart becoming an acutely painful throb.

———

HUMANS. WHAT DID SHE NEED THEM FOR?

Okay, so they made great dance partners, like the five men who surrounded her on the club's dance floor. While most Shifters went to a place called Coolers on the north side of town, Lindsay didn't want to face her friends tonight. They'd ask her coyly where Xav was, and less coyly—*what is going on with you two?*

Lindsay didn't want to talk about it. She didn't know what to talk about, anyway. Xav obviously wasn't in a rush to settle down or even be semi-serious about a relationship.

She knew what *she* wanted, but lately Lindsay had started to wonder why she was wasting her time. She was already past her hundredth year, well beyond her Transition from cub to adulthood, the age she'd become old enough to take a mate.

There were plenty of male Shifters in Shiftertown, because the ratio of females to males was low. That meant Lindsay could be choosy, but it was looking less and less likely that her main choice—a sexy human—was in her future.

Besides, she didn't simply want a mate, someone to bear cubs with. Lindsay wanted what all Shifters did—to find the mate bond, that powerful, magical tie that tethered Shifters to their beloved. Every flutter in her chest when she was around Xav made hope leap high that she was forming it with him.

Then Xav would get mad at her, like tonight, or else they'd have a blast together and say goodnight, nothing moving past lighthearted fun, and Lindsay's hopes would die once more. Whether Xav could even form the mate bond with Lindsay—or any Shifter for that matter—was a question she hesitated to explore. The answer might devastate her.

Her five current dance partners never sensed her inner turmoil. They only saw a lady in a blue glittery dress ready to have fun.

Lindsay tried to let herself enjoy watching the guys show off, busting out their moves, trying to get close. They were hoping for payoff, which she should tell them wasn't going to happen.

She could have her pick of them, but she held off, because she only wanted Xav.

Lindsay hid a sigh. She was going to have to rethink her whole life.

That one had prospects, Lindsay decided, studying her coterie. He was dark haired and blue eyed, filled out his shirt nicely, and didn't wear a wedding ring or have a tan line where he'd taken one off. He looked like he'd be fun and not bother her afterward.

So, why wasn't Lindsay sashaying over, cutting him out of the herd, taking him someplace nice and relieving her ever-growing mating need?

Lindsay forced her feet to move in his direction. The guy

caught on, beaming her a wide smile. Not as nice as Xav's million-kilowatt smile, but whose could be?

Her restlessness wanted this, but her heart was still torn, as was the wildcat that lay within her.

When had she decided it was Xav or nothing?

Lindsay had just convinced herself to let it go, run off with this guy for what fun she could have, and move on, when her phone buzzed.

On any other night, she might ignore it, but Cassidy, who was the second-ranking Shifter in all Shiftertown, sometimes asked Lindsay to help out in whatever crisis was going down. Plus, Cassidy was carrying another cub, and though she had a while to go yet, she relied on Lindsay more and more these days.

It said a lot about Lindsay's state of mind that she welcomed solving the problems of contentious Shifters to a night of impulsive shagging.

She lifted her forefinger at the guy, telling him to give her a second, and slid her tiny phone from the small pocket in her dress.

It was a text from Xav, and contained only one word.

Help.

CHAPTER THREE

W here is he?" Lindsay demanded.

Diego Escobar met Lindsay's question with grim hardness in his eyes.

They stood on a dark and cold highway north of Las Vegas, stars sharp in the early February sky. While daytime temps could rise into the sixties and sometimes seventies, nights remained in the low forties, especially in this area, where the land started to rise toward high mountains.

When she'd seen Xav's text, Lindsay had immediately abandoned the club and called Diego, to find that Diego had already realized Xav was missing.

"I have a tracker on him," Diego had informed Lindsay on the phone. "We keep them on each other during a mission. He never came back to the office tonight, so I reactivated it."

"Great, then you know where he is."

Diego's silence had Lindsay in her car, screeching out onto the road to head toward DX Security's offices.

"Not exactly," Diego had finally answered. "I'm texting you a map of his last known location. Meet me there."

Lindsay's phone wasn't state-of-the-art, as Shifters were

only allowed older technology, but it was enough for Lindsay to find the place Diego meant.

Though Las Vegas was a teeming city that continued to grow each year, beyond its edges the desert got empty and dark very fast. On a stretch of road past the turnoff to Mount Charleston, Diego waited for Lindsay to pull onto the shoulder behind his SUV.

She'd passed exactly one car on her journey, and it had been heading the other way. Now she and Diego stood alone in the endless darkness, Diego's flashlight the only illumination. Not that Lindsay needed much light. The night was clear, and stars and the quarter moon were plenty for her cat's vision.

"I found this here." Diego held up a round device, no bigger than a button. "We don't bother using phone apps, because phones are the first things gotten rid of. This was sewn inside his shirt."

A cold lump formed in Lindsay's chest. The fact that Diego held the tracker meant someone had ripped it from Xav's clothes. They'd have thrown away his bulletproof vest as well, if he'd still been wearing it when he was nabbed.

"Who did this?" Lindsay asked, though she knew Diego would have already told her if he'd known.

Diego shook his head and held the device out to Lindsay. "Can you help?"

He meant, could Lindsay pick up a scent and find Xav? She didn't know—if they'd taken him away in a vehicle at great speed, then no. Scent only revealed so much.

But she'd have a damn good try.

"Let me stash my clothes," Lindsay said. "Look after my phone for me?"

Diego took it without a word. Lindsay returned to her car and skimmed off her jacket, dress, and heels while Diego politely kept the flashlight trained elsewhere.

She put the car between herself and any chance passing vehicle, dragged in a breath, and sought her inner wildcat.

Lindsay didn't like shifting too many times in one day, because each attempt grew progressively difficult and more painful. This was for Xav, she reminded herself as she grimaced with her struggle.

After a few agonizing minutes, she was fully cat. Lindsay shook herself out and trotted toward Diego on her padded lynx paws, the cold fading into insignificance.

Diego held out the tracking device, and Lindsay took a long sniff. Not that she needed to learn Xav's scent—it was already ingrained in her. The Shifter in her knew that walking away from him forever was not an option.

Lindsay tested the air, letting her wildcat senses take over.

There were so many scents on the wind—dust, coyotes on the prowl, the tang of exhaust that lingered on the highway, and strongest of all, Diego and his concern. Lindsay inhaled, analyzed what she smelled, and sorted the odors into neat categories. She was good at it, one of the best scenters in Shiftertown, which was one reason Cassidy counted on her so much.

She couldn't find Xav's scent, to her dismay, other than what was on the tracker or clung to Diego from daily contact with his brother.

But she knew Xav was out there.

Which made no sense. Lindsay couldn't simply follow someone's presence, as a psychic human might, or the very magical being called Ben, or special and gifted Shifters like Tiger.

Something came to her, though, like a tendril through the darkness, telling her that Xav was *that way*.

Lindsay gave the tense Diego a *follow-me* look and set off north across the desert.

———

XAV KEPT HIS EYES SHUT, FEIGNING UNCONSCIOUSNESS.

His captors had sprung upon him in the darkness of the arena parking lot after Diego and the others had departed, as Xav had walked confidently to his car, the only one left in the lot.

He'd fought, but there'd been three men, strong and competent, who'd quickly divested Xav of weapons. They hadn't been members of the gang Xav and Diego had just arrested—Xav had never seen them before.

The punch behind his ear had stunned him but not completely knocked him out. Xav had readily folded up, pretending it had. This forced his captors to heave his limp body around and also allowed Xav to listen to them.

They'd ripped his phone from his hand, after he'd been able to send the one-word text to Lindsay, and tossed it into the nearest dumpster. He'd already removed his bulletproof vest as he'd made for his car, and they'd found and ripped the tracker from the hem of his shirt. Next, they'd zip-tied Xav's ankles and then his wrists behind him and stuffed him into the covered bed of a pickup.

They headed far into the desert, leaving paved highways behind. The air lost the taint of the city and took on the crisp dryness of sparsely vegetated open ground coupled with the dust the pickup raised in its wake.

No one drove a person out this far for any good reason. In the dense, trackless desert, it might be months before a dead body was found—or the remains of one, anyway. Buzzards and coyotes would be glad of the easy meal.

These morbid thoughts didn't cheer him, but Xav wasn't about to go down without a fight. Diego would track Xav as far as he possibly could, and he'd recruit help. Xav simply had to stay alive until Diego found him.

The zip ties were tight, but he worked to loosen them as much as he could while he lay alone in the rocking darkness.

The truck was an older model but not too decrepit to navigate the winding dirt road and ungraded washes. After a long time of bumping and jolting, the pickup halted.

From Xav's calculations—the time he'd counted in his head, plus the relatively slow speed a road like this would need—they'd gone about twenty miles off the highway.

His captors yanked open the truck's tailgate and hauled Xav out. They dragged him through dense darkness into some kind of building and dropped him on the floor. Two of the guys remained with him, leaving the third outside as a guard.

Light illuminated a cramped space, Xav saw through barely-open eyes. Someone slammed a door, cutting the freezing draft that had blown in with them. Now it was just cold.

Xav slumped against the wall where he'd landed, keeping his hands behind his back. The zip ties on his wrists no longer impeded him, but he'd not move until the time was right.

The large man who crouched over him had thick brown hair and a hard face. He was human, not Shifter, which was to Xav's advantage. Humans were much easier to lie to.

The man smacked Xav's cheeks, stinging blows meant to wake him. Xav mumbled and groaned, then gasped when a second man, much thinner than his companion, emptied half a bottle of water into his face.

Xav blinked and shook his head as though he returned to awareness slowly, as someone who'd been out an hour or so would do.

He cracked open his eyes. "Waste of water, dude," he said to the wiry man.

"Might be all you get," the big man informed Xav. "You answer me, and maybe we'll let you walk back to town."

An electric camp lantern lit the room they occupied, which was very small and made of metal and chipped concrete, its ceiling low. The door, newer than the rest of the building, closed off any sound from outside. Not that there would be much, but they should have heard wind through the dry plants and the yip of distant coyotes.

Xav had a feeling he knew where he was, which was good. Diego would also know this place. They'd explored it more than once as irresponsible adolescents.

At least, Xav had been irresponsible. Diego had been a workaholic since he'd been about three and had only softened with his mating to Cassidy and the birth of his adorable daughter. Xav knew Cassidy was expecting again, though it was early days.

Xav continued to feign grogginess. "Answer what?"

"Where is she?" the big man demanded.

Great. An asshole who wouldn't speak in clear sentences. He'd expect Xav to know what he was talking about and beat on him if Xav protested that he didn't.

Xav was very familiar with such bullies, having grown up around them. He'd survived when young by being cute and when older by being charming. Bullies were confused by charm.

"Which she?" Xavier managed a grin. "There are so many out there. Most of them sweet. Can you narrow it down?"

"She works for you."

DX Security employed a number of women who did all sorts of jobs, from extraction team members to accountants. Xav had the feeling he knew who the guy was talking about, though.

"Emma? She doesn't really work *for* us. More like with us,

when she feels like it. Are you sure you want to mess with her? She can kick serious ass."

"Not Shields. The other woman. The Shifter."

Holy fucking shit, he was talking about Lindsay.

Xav's heart banged while he tried to keep up his inane grin and pretended befuddlement. Lindsay could also kick serious ass and take out a human man as big as this one without much effort. Xav was always amazed at her strength and quickness, as he had been in the arena earlier.

But there were three of them—no, four. There was another guy in here, one who stayed in the shadows, which Xav didn't like. The man beyond the lantern light seemed familiar, and Xav busily wracked his brains to remember why.

Four men tracking down Lindsay and subduing her with a tranq dart was not a scenario Xav desired. Why they wanted her, Xav didn't know.

Not that it mattered. It wasn't going to happen.

"Shifter?" he asked as though bewildered. "If you mean my sister-in-law, she doesn't work for us." Not officially, but these guys didn't need to know details. "And you don't want to mess with her either."

If Lindsay was tough, Cassidy was a force of nature. Cass and Diego had once taken on a rogue Shifter and his band, demolishing his headquarters and rescuing a bunch of his captives and their cubs. Cass had also rescued Xav in that adventure, and he'd come out of it with a broken arm and admiration for Diego's new mate.

"Not your brother's bitch," the large man stated. "The one you're screwing. Bring her to us." He held out a cell phone, not Xav's and probably not his own. A burner, most likely.

Xav didn't bother to protest that he and Lindsay weren't screwing. Xav wished they were, but relationships with Shifters were complicated.

Diego's sister-in-law, Iona, had explained to Xav that if Lindsay didn't form what was known as the mate bond with him, then no matter how great a time they had together, nothing would be permanent. Regardless of her feelings for Xav, the moment Lindsay mate bonded with another Shifter, she'd be gone. Forever. Not a damn thing Xav could do about it.

That fact had made Xav hesitate. Sure, he could settled for a casual relationship, as he had in the past with other women, but he knew he didn't want casual with Lindsay.

And so, they kept each other at arm's length and then argued about it, as they had tonight.

Xav stared at the phone as though he'd never seen one before. "She's not going to answer if she doesn't know it's me. What do you want her for, anyway? Are you thinking to hire a Shifter woman to break heads for you? That can backfire big time, you know."

The shadowy man in the back finally stepped forward. "Watch him," he advised the other two. "He's tricky."

Xav's memory abruptly dredged up the guy's identity, and it did not make him happy.

His name was AC Parkes. Xav and Diego had arrested him for gun running years ago, when they'd been police detectives. After a lengthy trial, in which both Xav and Diego had taken the witness stand multiple times, AC had been carted off to prison.

He'd aged in the last fifteen years, now balding with graying brown hair and a grizzled close-cut beard, but he still bulked with muscle, and his light brown eyes held the same hardness.

AC stood for Andrew Colin, but he'd shot people who called him that. AC had been put away for a long stretch, and Xav had figured that had been that.

Obviously he was out again, and he wanted Lindsay. Nothing was adding up to anything good.

The larger thug balled a hefty fist. "Tell us where she is."

"Like I'd know." Xav managed to scowl at him. "If she's not home, she's out somewhere. Lindsay goes her own way."

The statement was the truth. Tonight, after Xav had pissed her off for scaring the shit out of him, Lindsay had stomped away, heading who knew where.

Xav had texted her because she was at the top of his favorites list and the easiest to reach before they'd grabbed his phone from him. He assumed she'd call Diego and pass off the task of rescuing him, if Lindsay paid attention to his plea at all. Whenever she got angry at Xav, she could stay mad for weeks.

The wind must have strengthened outside, because the door rattled in its frame. The door was an add-on, something from a building supply store, with nowhere near the resilience of the rest of the structure. *That* had been constructed to withstand a nuclear blast.

Xav and Diego had played here when they were kids, having imaginary adventures both on earth and in outer space. This little building had made a decent spaceship. Xav knew it had no back door or any windows. Having no other way in but the front entrance made for good protection but also turned the little building into a trap.

AC gestured to the rangy guy. "Help Rick check the perimeter."

The wiry guy nodded reluctantly and slipped outside. He was obviously not pleased to be ordered around, but he didn't disobey.

Wise. AC wasn't someone who took insubordination lightly.

A cold draft blew in when the rangy man opened the door then cut off when he slammed it.

Xav's thoughts churned rapidly. His plan to sit tight and wait for Diego had changed when he'd realized AC was his true captor. AC could kill Xav on a whim, leaving his dead body for Diego to find. Xav would have to get out of this himself.

The zip ties on Xav's wrists no longer restrained him, but he would still have to disentangle himself from them and the ones on his ankles, disarm the big guy, and use him as a shield against AC. A lot to coordinate. Xav had to choose his moment.

The big man continued to hold out the burner phone they wanted Xav to use. "I can't call anyone with my hands tied," Xav told him.

He'd have to make his move when the big guy turned him around to cut the zip ties, especially when they realize he'd loosened them. Now or never.

Another gust of wind rattled the door, followed by something that sounded like a boulder banging into it.

"Check that out," AC told the large man. "Leave the phone."

The big guy did *not* want to go out and find out what had happened to his partners, but like his thinner colleague, he hesitated to risk AC's wrath.

He laid the phone on the dirt floor and hauled himself to his feet, his head nearly touching the ceiling once he straightened all the way. He opened the door, bringing in another cold gust, glanced around into the darkness, and tentatively stepped out.

A blast of wind caught the door and slammed it for him.

Xav was left with AC, who studied him closely. Xav flashed him a grin that held more confidence than he felt.

"You gonna risk untying me? Now that it's just us?"

"No." AC crouched out of Xav's reach and lifted the phone. "What's her number?"

It wouldn't help Xav to lie about that so he relayed it. AC tapped the numbers, put the phone on speaker mode, and held it close enough to Xav so he could talk.

After three rings, Lindsay's chirpy and at the same time sexy voice filled the small space. "This is Lindsay. Leave a message."

AC swiped the phone off before Xav could speak. "We'll try again later."

Xav shrugged. "Whatever."

Xav had managed to hide his surprise at Lindsay's voice-mail greeting. She didn't have voicemail—most Shifters still weren't allowed it. Which meant Lindsay had actually answered and pretended she hadn't.

Because she hadn't recognized the number? Or because she was up to something else?

Another muffled bang sounded, this time on the roof.

"Wind really blows around here," Xav said cheerfully. "Up to gale force sometimes. Dust storms like you wouldn't believe."

"I know. I grew up here." AC removed a pistol from a back holster and pointed it at Xav. "Get out there and see what's going on."

"Oh, sure, if the first two landing parties got obliterated, beam a third down into the same unknown situation and see what happens to them."

AC scowled. "What?"

"Sorry, my niece is really into *Star Trek*. She's three and stares at the shows for hours. Old ones, new ones, and every-thing in between. My sister-in-law says Captain Picard is her babysitter."

Apparently, AC had never watched TV in his life. His expression didn't change as he hauled Xav to his feet.

Xav kept his hands tucked behind him. If he tried to over-power AC while AC's firearm pressed right against Xav's ribs,

Xav would die. He'd wait until he got outside and then use the darkness and whatever was distracting the other guys to get the hell out of there.

AC opened the door and shoved Xav out, stepping back into the shelter of the building, pistol still trained on Xav.

Before Xav had time to look around, someone tackled him, carrying him several feet from the vault before he hit the ground. The large door slammed in AC's face and a metal bar slid across it, trapping the man inside.

Xav rolled onto his back, tossing away the zip ties and bracing against the heavy, warm object on his chest.

He looked up into the green eyes of a large lynx, who put her furry paw on his chin. She was a beautiful cat, but the look in her eyes told Xav to stay down if he knew what was good for him.

What could Xav do? He gave in.

Good choice, because it kept him out of the way of the horde of men and animals who swarmed up on top of the building and tore off its roof.

CHAPTER FOUR

Xav was alive and well, Lindsay told herself. His strong body was beneath hers, his melting smile bathing her in gladness. He had a few bruises on his face, but that was all. It could have been so much worse.

Lindsay should be reassured, but her heart continued to race with sickening fear.

When she'd seen his kidnapper train the gun on Xav as he walked out the door, she'd sprung from her hiding place where she'd half-shifted to answer the phone Diego had held out to her, and taken had Xav out of the way. She'd leapt sooner than she was supposed to, but to hell with the plan. Lindsay wouldn't risk Xav getting hurt so Diego could execute his perfect strategy.

She knew Xav would want to jump up and rush back into the thick of it, maybe getting hurt, so she rested her entire weight on him and willed him to stay down.

Xav obeyed, to her surprise.

Behind her, she heard Bear Shifter Brody's big voice inside the now roofless building. "Nice Glock. Too bad I hate guns." Then a crackling sound as Brody broke the pistol into shards.

Three other Shifters hauled the lead bad guy out of the open door and dragged him to face Diego.

His lackeys lay subdued in the darkness—Lindsay'd had fun tripping them up as they came out so Diego and a couple of DX Security men could grab them. Leaping up onto the roof and jumping around on it had been fun too.

Diego had negated Lindsay's idea to simply run into the building, take the guys out, and haul Xav to safety. No, they had to follow the plan.

She'd known there were three inside with Xav from their distinct scents. Diego had verified this using a camera that registered heat signatures—he always had to see things for himself.

Interestingly, Diego had only been able to register the heat signatures through the door. The rest of the building was too thick or shielded or something.

Once the leader was thoroughly searched and disarmed, his wrists bound, Lindsay quietly stepped off Xav and loped away into the darkness.

She located the backpack Diego had stashed for her under a creosote bush, struggled with the shift to her human self, and then donned the shirt and jeans she'd worn to leave the arena stakeout. So much for the party dress.

Lindsay rejoined the others, backpack slung over her shoulder. Diego and Xav had the four bad guys lined up, the scene illuminated by electric lanterns. The lackeys looked either scared or angry, but their leader was impassive. He was the dangerous one.

"So you decided to kidnap my brother," Diego was saying in that calm way of his, which meant trouble wasn't far behind. "You didn't think I'd come after him?"

"I was pretty sure you would," the leader said. "Counting

on it, in fact. I thought you'd be alone, though. Or maybe with just her." He nodded at Lindsay in a way she didn't like. "You and your brother were always tight and didn't rely on anyone else."

Xav's warm voice rumbled. "Things have changed."

"Yep," Diego acknowledged quietly. "Now when we work, we bring plenty of backup."

He didn't mean just the DX Security men in black fatigues, in plain sight in the circle of light. He meant the Shifters who loomed in the darkness, none of them in the best mood.

Only Brody, in human form, couldn't stop grinning at the leader, a gleeful twinkle in his dark eyes. But then, Bears.

"Do we have to have a conversation right now?" Graham, the joint Shiftertown leader and head of most of its Lupines, snarled from the shadows. "I'm freezing my balls off out here."

"If you're uncomfortable, so is he," Diego said in his cool tones. "Talk to me, AC. Why in the hell did you think kidnapping Xav was a good idea?"

Lindsay rested her on arm on Xav's shoulder. She was still mad at him, in theory, but right now she was too relieved he was all right to keep away from him.

"What does AC stand for?" Lindsay asked Xav with nonchalance. "Air Conditioner?"

Xav chuckled as the man called AC shot Lindsay a glower. "Something like that," Xav answered.

"I took him, because I wanted to get your attention," AC stated. "Let me borrow the cat Shifter, and I'll leave all of you alone."

He pinned a stare on Lindsay, and Lindsay stiffened. "*Borrow* me? What the fuck?"

Xav's amusement vanished. "You touch her, and you'll be a dead man before you know what hit you."

Lindsay took a step forward. "What will hit you is four sets of cat claws in your face."

"I don't want to touch her," AC said with an irritation that matched Graham's. "I want her to do something for me. Nothing sexual," he added rapidly.

Lindsay planted her hands on her hips. "You couldn't just *ask* me? You had to grab Xav and drag him and half of Shiftertown out into the desert?"

AC turned to address her as though they were the only two in the circle of light. "You think if I approached you on the street or at your club, you'd talk to me? Or that all these Shifters would let me near you? They're very protective of their women."

And the ladies were very protective of their men, Lindsay wanted to snarl. Humans didn't understand that it went both ways.

"I've been watching you," AC went on in a way that made Lindsay shiver. "You and Xav go out a lot. I figured if he called you, or got his brother to bring you to me in exchange, then we could have a talk."

Because AC believed Diego would value his brother's life far above Lindsay's. Which might be true—Lindsay wasn't certain how Diego felt about her—but again, the statement proved that AC didn't understand Shifters. The ones around him were now growling menacingly.

AC didn't understand Diego either. "I'd never have made an exchange like that," Diego said. "Why aren't you in prison, AC? Want to head back?"

"I served my sentence. Done." AC dusted off his palms. "I'm not on parole—I did the whole thing. You let me ask Lindsay this favor, and you'll never see me again."

Lindsay knew she should scoff and head back to the waiting SUVs, taking Xav with her, and ignore the man. But the curiosity that was her besetting sin held her back.

"Why me?" she asked. "Brody's bigger. Than everyone," she couldn't help adding.

Brody nodded, un-offended. "Pretty much."

"I don't need big." AC's mouth tightened, as though he barely held on to his patience. "I need fast and cunning. Of all the Shifters I've seen around, that's you."

"Cunning?" Lindsay repeated. "I'm going to take that as meaning smarter than most."

Xav was next to her again, his shoulder touching Lindsay's. "I don't care what kind of Shifter you're looking for, you're not getting one. Not Lindsay, not any of them."

"Shit, you're arrogant, Escobar," AC snapped. "You and your brother both. This is between me and the lady cat. You and your extraction team can go away."

"Not gonna happen," Xav said. "We're taking you and *your* team to the local police, or maybe the county sheriff—whosever jurisdiction we're in—for kidnapping, assault, and stalking."

"At least let him tell us what he wants me for," Lindsay broke in. "I have to know." She glared at Graham. "And I don't want to hear any Lupines saying that curiosity killed the cat."

A few rumbles told her that, yes, some had been about to express that opinion.

Diego's men already surrounded AC, but Graham now got behind the man and hemmed him in. Graham was far more intimidating than Diego's guards could ever be, and AC finally looked nervous.

"I need her to find someone for me," he said.

"Find who?" Lindsay asked before anyone else could speak.

"My brother."

The Shifters, including Lindsay, went quiet. Shifters could smell a lie, and the scent coming off AC indicated he spoke the truth.

If any request would get a Shifter's attention, it was this one. Shifters were all about family.

Lindsay's own household was small, consisting of her mom and dad—Leah and Martin—and herself, as Lindsay had been an only cub. Moving to the Las Vegas Shiftertown, however, had tied Lindsay to many others she considered family now—Cassidy and Diego, Eric and Iona, their collective cubs, Brody and his brother and mom, and now their mates. Even Graham and his unruly Lupines had become part of the fabric of her life.

Shifters took a threat to a person's family seriously, even if that person was heinous.

Diego sent AC a conceding nod. "We'll talk about this someplace else."

AC didn't argue or even look dismayed that Diego wasn't about to release him. He shrugged impassively. "Let my guys leave. They only did what I told them. I didn't give them a choice."

"Mm, I'll think about it." Diego jerked his head toward AC's henchmen waiting in the dark. "Bring them," he ordered his men.

The DX Security guys and Graham and his Lupines started herding AC and his subdued thugs toward the road and waiting vehicles.

Lindsay blew out a relieved breath once they'd all passed and turned to Xav. "You should go home and rest. Recover from this."

Xav sent her an incredulous look. "While you do what? Watch Diego interrogate AC?"

"Of course," Lindsay said, as though it should be obvious. "He asked for my help specifically. I want to know why." She laced her arm through Xav's, running her fingers along his biceps. "Then maybe I can come over and help you heal."

Xav didn't soften under her touch. "What's going to

happen is *you* are going back to Shiftertown and staying put. I don't like that AC singled you out, and I don't care about any sob story about his brother. The man can't be trusted. I don't want you near him."

"Then shouldn't we find out what he really wants?" Lindsay asked in surprise.

"Yes, *I* should. And Diego. I'll tell you all about it, I promise."

"Wait, you're saying you're going with Diego now?" Lindsay demanded. "Even though you've been beat up, kidnapped, and stuffed into this place—whatever it is—in the middle of the desert?"

"They didn't hurt me that much. Irritated me, mostly." Xav's bruised face belied the words, though he wasn't sagging in pain, and the arm she held was strong. "And it's a bank vault."

Xav gently slid from Lindsay's grasp and started for the distant road, where SUVs were sputtering to life. Headlights swept arcs into the darkness, taillights reddening the dust and dried grasses.

Lindsay jogged to catch up with him. "It's a what?"

"A bank vault," Xav answered without stopping. "Built by a manufacturer to demonstrate that his vaults could survive a nuclear blast. Back when this was a testing area, a few people shut themselves inside the vault and waited for a nuclear bomb to detonate nearby."

Lindsay gaped at him. "Are you shitting me? Were they nuts?"

Xav shrugged his broad shoulders. "It worked. They survived. The door blew off but the walls and roof stood. No one's ever come to tear the vault down and take it away."

Lindsay stared back at the tiny building, standing mutely in the starlight, a testimony to the vast destruction that had been developed in this remote place.

She knew it had been many years ago, and *probably* the radiation had dispersed by now, but she shivered and hurried after Xav to the warm and waiting vehicles.

———

XAV HELD IN HIS IRRITATION AS LINDSAY FOLLOWED HIM INTO DX Security's offices, which lay on Desert Inn Road not far from Boulder Highway.

Lindsay had ignored Graham's order that she should get into the SUV heading back to Shiftertown with his Lupines. He'd assured her that one of his wolves would drive her car home for her, but Lindsay had walked past him, wind ruffling her shoulder-length, light golden hair, and climbed into her driver's seat.

"No way am I letting a Lupine drive my car, Graham," she'd said, then slammed the door.

Graham might be a joint leader of Shiftertown, but Lindsay wasn't required to obey him. She only had to do what Eric, her own leader, said, and Eric wasn't here.

Xav had made for her car so he could at least keep arguing with her as they drove back, but Lindsay had glided away before he could reach it.

He understood why she'd resisted going home, Xav told himself when she waltzed into DX's offices. AC had singled her out, and Lindsay needed to know why. Xav knew *he* could not have gone tamely home and waited for a phone call to fill him in.

One contingent of DX men had taken the three thugs who'd grabbed Xav to the police. All three had outstanding warrants, Xav discovered as he'd looked them up on the drive back to town.

AC, however, came to DX Security with them. Diego wasn't ready to turn him over yet.

When Lindsay tried to follow Diego into the interrogation room, Xav seized her by the arm and steered into the chamber next door. Here, a thick glass window shielded them but would let them watch and hear the questioning.

Lindsay glared at Xav and jerked from his grip as he shut the door.

"Don't bother railing at me," Xav said in a hard voice. "I'm not letting you in there with AC. He has no reservations about killing people who get in his way. His guys tied me up and stuffed me into the back of a truck, even though I'm trained to not let that happen."

Lindsay released the breath she'd drawn for the argument in a long, slow exhale. "Fine. I'll stay behind the window. There's no room in there, anyway."

True, the chamber was crowded with the large AC behind a table, plus Graham, Brody, two human guards, and Diego.

Diego knew how to design an interrogation room. It was small enough to be claustrophobic, with no windows except the mirrored one that the captive would know others watched him through. Its electronically locked door was solid, though Xav had a keycard in case he and more guards needed to rush in.

AC's wrists were zip-tied in front of him but Diego let him rest his hands on the table, no extra restraints. Brody and Graham were deterrent enough.

"Tell me something," Lindsay said to Xav. "Why did you get so mad at me when I helped out at your bust, but it was okay for Diego to bring a bunch of Shifters along to fight only four guys?"

"Because the one at the arena was an official police sting," Xav answered without having to consider. "This is personal, and Diego didn't know exactly what he'd be dealing with. Besides, Diego would never let a Shifter touch a human captive."

Lindsay sent him a steady stare, not indicating whether she was satisfied with the answer. She silently turned to watch as Diego took the seat across from AC, sitting in his upright but relaxed way.

"All right, talk to me," Diego said. "Why did you want Lindsay, in particular, to help you find your brother?"

"Like I said, I need someone small and quick." AC cast a glance at the hulking Brody, whose Shifter was a massive grizzly, and Graham, a wolf who was nearly as massive. "Someone no one will see coming."

Brody sent him a toothy grin. "They'd see me, all right."

"You believe someone has taken your brother hostage?" Diego asked, ignoring Brody. "Do you have evidence of this? Did they ask for a ransom?"

"No, no ransom. No one would be that stupid." AC made an impatient noise. "When I was inside, my brother, Dean, who doesn't have a lot of sense, started running with some very bad people. He's in deep with them now, and they won't let him go. He doesn't understand that they're using him, and that in any risky situation, it's going to be him who gets killed. I want someone who can pinpoint his location so I can bring in my own extraction team and haul him out."

"Sounds like you know exactly where he is," Diego said. "If you think you're sending Lindsay in like a canary down a mine shaft, think again."

"I'm not going down a mine shaft," Lindsay said softly, wrinkling her nose. "Too dirty."

"It's a metaphor," Xav said.

They'd drifted closer together to listen to the questioning, though Xav didn't know if Lindsay realized it. She didn't move away at his correction, only rolled her eyes.

"I know it's a metaphor," she said. "I was joking."

"Sorry." Sometimes it was hard to fathom what Lindsay was thinking. "With AC, he might literally want you to go down an old mine shaft." Nevada's and nearby California's mountains were littered with them.

"Well, too bad for him." Lindsay remained close to Xav, which was as distracting as it was gratifying.

"I know where he *was*," AC was explaining to Diego. "These guys stay on the move. If I can get the Shifter to their last known location, maybe she can get a bead on them for me. And maybe sneak into their new hideout, when we find it, and make sure Dean is okay."

"Then you retrieve him," Diego finished. "Got it. What happens to Lindsay?"

AC shrugged. "I figure she can take care of herself. I once watched her ... discourage ... a couple of human guys who were bothering her in a club. Those dudes will leave her alone from now on. You know, when they can walk straight again."

Lindsay chuckled. "That was fun."

"You almost got arrested that night," Xav reminded her. "We barely got away before the cops arrived. We're lucky no one reported you to Shifter Bureau."

Lindsay lost her smile. "Don't take all the joy out of it."

Xav decided not to answer. She was right—it had been exhilarating to watch Lindsay swift-punch two men who had been all over her, cornering her the second Xav had stepped to the bar for more drinks. He'd returned to find Lindsay standing over two groaning assholes, and he'd had to drag her away when she wanted to stay and gloat.

Why couldn't they ever have a conversation without squabbling?

Because Xav had to let himself be fascinated by an unpredictable Feline Shifter. Who was even now at the door and zipping out into the hallway.

"Lindsay, what the hell?"

Xav realized, as he stormed after her, that she'd lifted the keycard to the interrogation room from his pocket. Damn it, he'd never felt a thing.

Lindsay was fast. By the time Xav caught up to her, she'd unlocked the door and let herself into the roomful of humans and Shifters.

"I'll do it," Lindsay announced and beamed a smile on AC. "For pay, of course. I'm not risking my life for nothing." She wrinkled her nose and fanned her face with her hand. "And, please, keep the door open, Diego. It truly stinks in here."

CHAPTER FIVE

L indsay knew Xav wanted to yell at her. She pretended to be interested in the dark streets rolling by outside the window while she braced herself for his anger.

Diego had relented to her acceptance of AC's task, saying Lindsay was her own person, and if she wanted a paying job from AC, that was her business. But—Diego insisted—she would use DX Security as her backup, essentially becoming an adjunct employee, or Diego would turn her over to Eric.

Diego played dirty. He knew Eric would lock Lindsay in her basement if she didn't do what Diego asked, recruiting Lindsay's parents to stand guard over her. Her mom and dad would agree with Eric and Diego and do it.

Lindsay had expected Xav to become all overbearing human male and suggest they lock her in her basement regardless, but he'd just stood there like a stone. Not a happy stone, but he hadn't argued with Diego or overridden his decision.

When they'd departed, Xav had guided Lindsay out to the parking lot and the black SUV that he drove for work. Her protest that her own car was sitting *right there* didn't deter him. He was taking her home, promising Diego would have her car delivered later.

Lindsay decided not to fight him on that. She trusted DX's guys with her car far more than Graham and his Lupines, and besides, she welcomed the chance to be alone with Xav, no matter how awkward the situation.

Now they were moving north through the city toward Shiftertown in absolute silence.

Even this far from the Strip and downtown, Las Vegas's nightlife bustled. Clubs were open, and Lindsay wished Xav would pull into one so she could work off her excess energy.

Xav was clearly not in the mood for dancing. He was furious, but he kept it in, as only he could. Diego got very active when he was mad, but Xav could become a wall.

Lindsay waited for Xav to say something—anything—but he remained stubbornly quiet until they pulled into Shiftertown and stopped in front of the small house Lindsay shared with her folks.

Across the strip of yard behind it lay Eric's house, home to Cassidy and Diego, Eric and Iona, and their collective brood of cubs. Lindsay loved visiting them, basking in the love and laughter that filled the rooms. Plus, Xav usually hung out there on his days off.

Her own house was quieter, though no less loving. Theirs was a small family but a close one.

"Why, Linds?" Xav finally spoke as Lindsay lingered, not wanting to open the door and leave him. "AC is bad news, and you can't trust him. Why don't you believe me?"

"I do believe you." Lindsay turned in the seat to face him, happy they were finally talking. "Who says I'm going to trust him? But is AC being a baddie a reason to let his brother suffer? I wouldn't if it was *my* brother. I don't have a brother, but I can imagine what it must feel like."

"So, compassion is driving you?" Xav's gaze was merciless,

piercing her bravado. "Or do you simply enjoy running headlong into danger?"

Lindsay shrugged. "Not much else to do around here, is there?"

Xav wasn't wrong, and she hated that. Lindsay excused her restlessness as wanting her independence, but she knew what she truly longed for. But the mate bond took its time, and it might have someone else in store for her altogether.

The uncertainty of it all drove her wild. Xav glaring at her accusatorially didn't help.

"This is between me and AC," Lindsay declared. "DX Security will be my backup, like Diego said. It's not really your decision, Xav. Good night."

She made herself turn away and thrust open the door. She hopped out, remembering at the last second to grab her backpack. She thought about how nervously she'd packed it tonight, worried for Xav and his dangerous mission and planning to celebrate with him afterward.

Lindsay slammed the door and turned to find Xav standing almost against her. How he'd moved so quietly, she didn't know. Her Shifter senses must have failed her in her agitation.

"Take this seriously, Linds," he said.

Lindsay had trouble concentrating on anything but Xav. His eyes were midnight dark, moonlight glowing in his sable hair. She loved his face, square and hard, the kindness in him almost hidden behind his toughness.

Xav must have expected her to answer, because he frowned when she didn't.

Lindsay tried to think of a lofty response, but before she could form words, Xav jerked her against him. She gaped up at him, startled by the fierce light in his eyes, the one that revealed the hard man beneath his lighthearted exterior.

Her heart hammered as he gazed down at her, unreadable as always. Lindsay, with her superior scent-sense usually knew what others were thinking, but never Xav.

Just when she thought he'd release her and turn away, Xav swiftly leaned to her and took her parted lips in a hard kiss.

Xav didn't kiss Lindsay often, but when he did it, he did it well.

His mouth commanded, compelling her to open to him, to kiss him as powerfully in return. The world melted as Lindsay's frustration dissolved on a wave of need.

She tasted the coffee he'd drunk at DX to stay awake, as well as his anger, and his lingering apprehension. Xav might have died tonight if things had gone differently, and he knew it.

Lindsay clutched at his jacket, wanting him closer. His body came against hers, the need tearing through both of them making itself known as a hard ridge against her abdomen.

The SUV behind Lindsay held her upright, its cold surface a stark contrast to Xav's warm strength. He pressed her against its door, hands on her shoulders, fingers biting.

She couldn't stop the yearning sound that escaped her throat. The SUV was waiting, and it had wide back seats ...

Abruptly, Xav broke the kiss. Lindsay gasped as he pulled away, she the agile cat struggling to retain her balance.

Xav gazed down at her with his starlit eyes, his breath coming fast. She couldn't read what he was thinking, couldn't scent it through the pounding in her head.

He stared at her for an interminable moment, then he turned on his heel, walked around the SUV, and climbed in without a word.

Lindsay stepped back, bereft, as Xav pulled away from the curb without acknowledging her. The SUV glided down the street, taillights flashing as he slowed for the corner.

Xav took the turn and was lost to sight, leaving Lindsay with her heart aching and her mouth tingling from that spectacular kiss.

———

Xav couldn't avoid Shiftertown if he wanted to. The very next day, after he'd tossed and turned all night, he was obligated to go back.

While he'd lain awake, his restless mind had spun pictures of Lindsay gazing at him with her sultry green eyes while he growled at her for being brave enough to rescue him —twice.

When he hadn't been buried in thoughts of her, he'd had unnerving flashbacks to the hours he'd spent as a captive, not knowing if he'd ever see Lindsay or his family again. He'd been certain Diego would come for him, but there'd always been a good chance Diego wouldn't make it before his captors grew impatient and shot him.

Diego and Lindsay *had* made it, he kept reminding himself. Xav had come out of the adventure with only a few scrapes and bruises.

Xav's conflicted emotions had propelled him from the SUV last night when Lindsay had climbed out in front of her house, because he hadn't wanted her to walk away. Instead of playing it cool and letting her go, he'd kissed her.

That kiss had been dangerous. Lindsay had softened to him, making Xav believe she'd surrender. They could spend a night enjoying each other, her returning kiss had promised, and behave sensibly again in the morning.

But no, Lindsay would always, *always* do exactly as she pleased. It didn't matter that she put herself into terrifying danger and made Xav sick with worry. She was a Shifter, and while Xav admired Shifters, they truly believed themselves invincible and were surprised when humans expressed concern for them.

That kiss had to be their last. Xav was done fighting with her.

After hours of sleeplessness, Xav had finally crashed, his body taking over and forcing him into recovery mode. Being knocked out, tied up in the back of a truck, and then threatened in a remote, aging bank vault took its toll.

The next morning was Sunday, and also the birthday of Callum, Eric and Iona's cub. Xav had been ostensibly invited by his three-year-old Trek-loving niece, Amanda, to attend Callum's party. Uncle Xav could never say no to Amanda, and so early afternoon saw him driving back to Shiftertown, this time in his silver Mustang, no work vehicle today.

Xav walked into Eric's house to find it packed. Cubs ran everywhere, in both human and animal forms, moving too rapidly to distinguish who was who. Xav heard Diego and Cassidy in the kitchen, as usual, because Diego was pretty much the cook for the entire family. Iona, a lovely woman with dark hair and ice-blue eyes, lithely ran after the cubs.

Eric Warden lounged on the sofa like the king cat he was, surveying his domain. Xav had come to know that the laid-back Eric was in fact very astute, knew who was doing what at all times, and could leap into action in a heartbeat.

The bears from next door were there, filling out the small room and spilling into the backyard. It was a mild day, in the high sixties, perfect for cooking out. Shane, Brody's brother, beamed his large grin on everyone. He was smug, now that he'd mated with Freya, a wolf-Shifter, and they were expecting a cub.

With them was Keira, a Lupine who'd until recently been feral. She still regarded everyone warily, though she relaxed when she was around the cubs.

Stuart Reid greeted Xav as he entered. Reid worked for

DX Security, but he wasn't Shifter. He was *dokk alfar*, he'd quickly correct anyone who called him a Fae, but other humans didn't realize he wasn't human. Reid had the handy skill of being able to teleport himself, and if things had gone worse last night, Diego might have deployed him.

Xav was just as glad he'd ridden out of the desert the conventional way. Teleporting with Reid was a stomach-churning experience.

The only person Xav didn't see in the crowded house was Lindsay. He thought he heard her voice mingling with Cassidy's, but by the time he made his way through the hordes in the living room and into the kitchen, she was gone.

Diego, in a long blue-and-green striped apron, threw a handful of chopped chiles into a pan sizzling on the stove. A Dutch oven on a back burner emitted the unmistakable savory odor of carnitas. Diego had learned his carnitas recipe from their mom, Juanita, and the result would be melt-in-the-mouth pork that was perfect rolled into a fresh tortilla, no need of any other seasoning or sauce.

Xav's love for carnitas was eclipsed by his frustration over Lindsay. He craned to peer out the back door, which he swore he'd heard slam as he'd slid through the crowd.

"She's gone," Cassidy informed him.

Tall, blond Cassidy turned her leopard stare on Xav, not without some sympathy.

Once upon a time, Diego's love for this woman had gotten Xav abducted by murderous feral bears and his arm smashed, but hey, anything for his bro's happiness, right?

"Who's gone?" Xav asked, trying to sound innocent. "That smells great, *hermano*." He gave Diego a friendly pat on the back. "Can't wait."

"Lindsay." Cassidy had a glass of water in her hand, another hint that she was pregnant. "She had to go home."

"Did she?" Xav gave up the pretense he hadn't been

looking for her. "She went out the back, because I came in the front?"

"Yes." Shifters were known for telling the painful truth.

"Shit," Xav said softly.

Cassidy tilted her head to indicate she wanted to speak to Xav in private before she sauntered to the back door and outside. She didn't mean to sashay, though Diego turned his head to watch her every stride. Felines always moved with lithe grace.

Xav walked out the door with much less finesse and slammed it behind him.

The open yard was filled with more cubs and Shifter adults. All of Eric's Shifters would come to celebrate their leader's son.

The birthday boy, Callum, who was two, ran around in the black leopard form he'd recently begun to shift into. Eric and Iona were both leopards, but they'd wondered if Callum would have his father's snow-leopard markings or the dark fur of his panther mother. The conundrum was over, which contributed to Eric's pleased-with-himself expression.

Several bear cubs chased Callum, followed by two boys who were twin wolves, all yelling at the top of their lungs.

Cassidy watched the cubs in fondness but the gaze she turned to Xav was steely. "What did you do?" she demanded once they'd found a relatively empty patch of ground in which to converse.

"To Lindsay?" Xav regarded his sister-in-law in exasperation. "I told her to stop racing into danger before she got herself killed. Excuse me for caring."

Cassidy's look turned pitying. "You told a Shifter woman to stay home while the menfolk go out and fight the battles?"

"Not exactly." Xav shrugged. "All right, maybe. But she scared the shit out of me last night. She followed us to a bust, and then she accepted a deal with a seriously bad—I mean *bad*—man. She didn't seem to think there was anything wrong with that." He let out breath. "I guess I don't know anything about Shifters."

"No, you don't know anything about *women*." Cassidy gave him a smile. "You try your best."

"Thanks a lot, Cass. What do I do to make it right?"

"Do you still want her to back off this thing with AC Parkes? I know what it's about. Diego told me." Diego told Cassidy everything, so her declaration wasn't a surprise.

"AC can't be trusted," Xav said with conviction. "I feel bad for his brother, yes, but DX Security can extract him if necessary. We're experts at it. I don't want Lindsay to get caught up in bad shit and hurt."

"I don't want her hurt either." Cassidy studied Xav in her unnerving cat way. "Shifter women don't stay out of the battle, Xav. They're very protective of their mates and their families. Male Shifters need all the teeth and claws on their side they can get, and they know it."

"I'm not her mate," Xav said. Why did that statement make him feel empty? He'd never pictured himself settling down, which was why things worked with Lindsay. She was as adamantly free-spirited as he was.

"You're family," Cassidy said. "Maybe not literally, but Lindsay and I are best friends, which makes her a part of my family, and me a part of hers. I'm mated to Diego, and you're Diego's brother. We're all connected."

"Are you saying I'm dating my cousin?" Xav joked. "Don't go there, Cass."

"Very funny. You know what I mean. We're all close, and you two have a relationship, if a weird and undefined one. Lindsay's going to protect you, and you can't stop her. Preventing her means not letting her follow her instincts, which is a sure way to break things off for good."

"Hiring herself to AC for his possibly deadly mission has nothing to do with her protecting me," Xav pointed out.

"Maybe it does. You basically told Lindsay *not* to protect you, so she's trying to prove herself to you. Shifters aren't human, *hermano*. We'll never follow your rules, so don't try to impose them."

Cassidy absently touched the Collar around her throat, which, like Lindsay's was fake.

"Not my rules," Xav said quickly. "I hate what Shifter Bureau has done to you."

Cassidy lowered her hand. "I meant that a Shifter woman isn't going to act the way a human man wants her to." She shrugged. "We can't."

They were momentarily interrupted by three cubs—a bear, a snow leopard, and a wolf—who circled the two of them at an insane pace and then raced away again.

"I think I figured that out a long time ago." Xav's mood softened. Cubs had that effect on him. "The protective thing is why you stayed with me when that crazy bear and his followers grabbed me. You could have gotten away from them easily. Diego wasn't even your mate yet, and you had no obligation to me."

"He was my mate in my heart." Cassidy smiled, the love she had for Xav's annoying older brother shining in her eyes. "That means you were already my brother, and he couldn't be there to look out for you." Her gaze sharpened. "I thought you were unconscious for most of that."

"Not as much as I was going to let those bears think." Xav had learned that the tactic often worked, which was why he'd employed it last night. "I *wished* I'd been unconscious when Reid took me out of there." He shuddered.

Cassidy had rescued a female bear that day who was now mated to Reid. Piegi, the bear in question, sprinted by in pursuit of a cub just as Xav spoke.

"I'll tell Stuart you said thanks," Piegi called as she raced past.

Xav rolled his eyes. "I can't open my mouth around here. Are you going to tell Lindsay I feel bad for yelling at her, or are you going to make me do it myself?"

Cassidy smiled. "What do you think?"

Xav suppressed a sigh and squared his shoulders. "Wish me luck."

Cassidy could have said something snide about him not needing it if he did things right, but she only continued her warm smile.

Xav doubted she ever lost an argument to Diego.

Cubs swarmed around Xav as he started across the yard toward Lindsay's house, using him as a marker for turning around and racing the other way. Xav waved as the cubs screamed their greetings and farewells. Sometimes it was fun being an honorary uncle to Shifters.

Xav usually went straight to the back door when he jogged from Eric's house to see Lindsay, but today for some reason, he decided the front door would be best.

The houses on Lindsay's street were low and long, built in an era before air conditioning became the norm. Low ceilings, thick walls, and small windows kept rooms cool against the blasting sun. Where summer temps could reach a hundred and ten and more, retreating under deep porches and into dim interiors made sense.

Ruminating on mid-twentieth century architecture let Xav procrastinate about knocking at the door. Unfortunately, Shifters had great hearing, so before he raised his hand, the door opened, and Lindsay's mother gazed out at him.

Leah Cummings greatly resembled Lindsay, with the same golden hair and green eyes, though with a stateliness Lindsay hadn't aged into yet. Leah's eyes danced as much as her daughter's, and she possessed the same intense stare, as though she knew everything about a person at first glance.

Lindsay's mom and her dad, Martin, were both lynx Shifters. They'd mated in a time before Shifter species inter-mixed much, when different sorts of Felines still avoided each other. Technically, all Felines were Fae-cats, originally bred by the Fae in their distant world, but over the centuries, the Feline clans had each tended toward some type of wildcat.

"Hello, Xav," Leah greeted him, sounding neither forbidding nor welcoming. "I'm sorry, honey, but she says she doesn't want to speak to you. Ever again, I'm afraid."

CHAPTER SIX

X av wasn't extremely surprised at Leah's declaration. She watched him with eyes so like Lindsay's while Xav pondered what to do.

He could turn around and walk away, pretend he was glad Lindsay was ending things. Or he could not let Lindsay's anger stop him.

"Will you tell her I'm here to talk about the mission?" he asked.

Leah's expression softened. "I'll try. Martin's in the kitchen. Go say hello to him, and I'll send Lindsay in if she's willing."

There was nothing else Xav could do but take himself into the kitchen while Leah moved down the hall so lightly Xav never heard her go.

Martin Cummings sat over the remains of his lunch, but he rose and smiled at Xav when he walked in.

"Xavier. How are you?" Martin shook Xav's hand with his usual firmness.

Martin wasn't as tall as most other Shifters but he had a

large frame and broad, strong shoulders. His hair was darker than his wife's, but streaked with blond, exactly matching his fur in lynx form.

Martin worked as a carpenter for a human business that made custom-built furniture. He moved with the slow quietness of someone who created things with his hands, and performed every task, even carrying his lunch dishes to the sink, with easy deliberation. Xav often wondered how this man had produced a daughter who couldn't sit still for more than five minutes.

"How's your mom doing?" Martin asked as he rinsed dishes.

"Fine," Xav answered, his long-ingrained fondness for Juanita Escobar warming him. "She just got back from a cruise to the Caribbean with her friends. I don't want to know what they did out there. I didn't ask."

Martin chuckled. "She probably went into every kitchen at every restaurant and tried to teach them how to cook."

"One of her friends told me she tried that on the ship." Xav grinned. "Thought the food was too bland, and she wanted to pep it up."

"Your mom's a good woman." Martin turned off the water and dried his hands. "But very bossy."

"Tell me about it. I was the only kid on the block with a room so clean you could eat off the floor. She always said we might be poor but that didn't mean we had to be slovenly. I tease her about it whenever she leaves a plate on the table." Xav grimaced. "Which she then makes me pick up."

"Serves you right." Martin sent him a quiet smile. "How's work? And that brother of yours?"

Martin had never, ever discussed Lindsay with Xav, or asked his intentions, or lectured him about how to treat his daughter. His philosophy was to let Lindsay and Xav work things out between them, a mindset Xav was grateful for. In the meantime, Martin had hinted, there was no reason for them not to be friends.

A big regret Xav would have if he and Lindsay really did call it quits would be losing his camaraderie with Martin and Leah.

Martin offered Xav a beer, and the two of them sat down and chatted about Diego, DX Security, and their big bust of the gun-runners at the arena last night. Xav kept Lindsay's part in the takedown out of it and didn't bring up the kidnapping either. From the shrewd light in Martin's eyes, he knew all about it but saw no advantage in discussing it.

Voices signaled that Leah and Lindsay had emerged from the back of the house. Xav took a final sip of beer, nodded to Martin, and left the kitchen, his entire body tensing.

Lindsay had donned a tight pink sweater with a low neckline that made it difficult for Xav to focus on anything else. He forced himself to look away from her curvy and blood-heating body and smile his thanks at Leah. Leah sent him an encouraging nod and slipped past him into the kitchen.

Lindsay snatched up a jacket from a hook beside the door. "If you want to talk, let's do it outside."

"Sure." Xav kept his tone neutral. "There are a million cubs in the back, who will listen to every word. Want to go out for some lunch? Snack? Beer?"

"Let's just walk." Lindsay skimmed out the front door, swinging on the jacket as she went.

Xav followed and closed the door carefully behind him.

Lindsay might not be as tall as Cassidy, but she could certainly stride. Xav jogged to catch up to her then matched her pace as they moved down the street toward the open fields at the end of the block.

Most of Shiftertown was at the party today, but those

Shifters who weren't—mostly Graham's Lupines—lounged on porches on this pleasant afternoon. Xav spied Dougal, Graham's nephew and second-in-command, who was probably keeping an eye on the Lupines who resented Eric enough to cause trouble at a cubs' birthday party. Dougal lifted a hand in greeting as they went by, and Xav waved back.

Another Lupine growled at Lindsay but shut up quickly when Xav shot him a quelling look.

Xav wondered why Lindsay was taking a route straight through Graham's territory full of disgruntled wolves, but it was possible she paid no attention. When Lindsay had a goal in mind, she just went.

They emerged from the cluster of houses into open land on the north side of Shiftertown. A new housing development for humans was being built not far away, but the desert in between was still pristine, full of creosote and native grasses. To the west rose the snowy ridge that held Mount Charleston, to the north and east, where they'd been last night, lower mountains framed the horizon.

Lindsay took in the view for a few moments before she turned and faced Xav. "So, you're deigning to let me find AC's brother for him?" she asked without preliminary.

Xav forced his gaze not to drift to the enticing sweater. "Diego is setting up another meeting for you with him." He shrugged. "You're going to do this whether I like it or not, so I might as well help you. You know, to lessen your chance of getting killed."

Lindsay scowled. "I'm a Shifter, Xav. We're resilient."

"Sure, but not immortal. AC could still shoot you multiple times until you're dead."

"We're also smart, fast, and strong. I do know what I'm doing, and I don't need you babysitting me." Lindsay's eyes flashed. "In fact, you'll probably just get in the way."

Xav blew out an exasperated breath. "Linds, you don't

have to prove anything to me, all right?" he said, recalling Cassidy's words. "I know you're capable. I just worry about you. You enjoy taking your life into your own hands, and it scares the shit out of me."

Lindsay stared at him. "*Prove* myself to you? Why do you think this has anything to do with you?"

Xav blinked at her in surprise. He'd been following Cassidy's advice, but he realized abruptly that, in spite of his protests to himself, he'd been thinking of himself and Lindsay as a couple. As though what he did affected her, and what she did affected him. As though they thought about each other all the time.

It became clear, in this moment, that Xav was the one doing all the thinking. Lindsay was saying she'd answered AC's plea for reasons of her own, reasons that didn't involve Xav. Her question dealt his ego a deep blow, but wasn't that his own fault?

"Okay, I guess it *doesn't* have anything to do with me." Xav heard his words come out, grim and hard. "If you don't want to deal with me anymore, Linds, then that's fine. I'll leave you alone."

"I didn't say that," Lindsay answered swiftly.

"I can't do this halfway." Xav folded his arms, strengthening his resolve not to seize Lindsay and kiss her until they forgot about everything but their passion for each other. "Either let me in or shut me out. Completely."

Lindsay's lips parted. "Are you saying you want to break up with me?"

"How can we break up?" Xav demanded in exasperation. "We're not together."

A swallow moved in her throat. "No, I guess we're not."

Her answer hurt even more. Xav wasn't certain what he wanted her to say, or what *he* wanted to say back. It was all a mess, and he couldn't think anymore.

The snowcapped peaks in the background were beckoning. He longed to go to Mount Charleston and ski or snowboard until his thoughts untangled. He had season tickets for the lifts—he shouldn't let them go to waste.

Xav's first instinct was to ask Lindsay to come with him. They'd gone to the mountain together before, to relax in the lodge or throw snowballs at each other or simply look at the scenery in quiet contentment. Though Lindsay claimed she'd never been skiing before, she'd taken the runs with her natural cat grace, learning quickly.

Xav shut down the ache in his heart and gave her a terse nod. "All right then," he made himself say. "I'll see you, Linds."

He turned on his heel and walked away. His footsteps crunched on gravel, loud in the sudden quiet.

Did Lindsay call after him? Beg him to stay? Yell at him for being an idiot?

Nope. He heard utter silence behind him.

When Xav reached the first houses of Shiftertown, he couldn't resist turning back to gaze at Lindsay one last time. She really did look great in that sweater.

Only empty desert reached his eyes, along with bright blue sky, steep mountains in the distance, and wintry sunshine. Lindsay was gone, and Xav was alone.

XAV GRABBED HIS GEAR AND HEADED FOR THE SLOPES, HOPING the biting cold and concentration needed to not fall on his ass would calm him down.

Mount Charleston was crowded on this sunny afternoon and the powder on the runs was good. The lines to the lifts were tedious, though once Xav was riding up through the trees, he relaxed a little.

Not enough, though. As Xav glided down the hill, his body recalling how to balance on his skis, he remembered the last time he'd brought Lindsay to the mountain, and what a great time they'd had. The best he'd ever experienced, in fact.

Lindsay could easily be mistaken for a human, if she wore a cowled sweater to hide her Collar and controlled her wilder side. That day, she'd been adorable in her pink padded jacket and matching knit hat, and smoking hot too.

After a few runs, they'd had a cozy dinner at the lodge, snuggling together in a booth, enjoying kisses with their champagne.

Xav had driven them home in the dark, Lindsay's head on his shoulder. Their kiss goodnight outside her house had been memorable, with promises of heat to come.

Lindsay had parted from him reluctantly, giving him a wave from the porch before going in. Xav had driven away, burning up inside, because the hottest girl in Shiftertown still lived with her parents.

Xav snapped back to the present, plowing to a halt at the end of the hill before he ran into another skier who'd lingered on the trail. He shook himself and pushed away, removing his skis instead of joining the line at the lift again.

The winter sky was darkening, and he knew Diego would soon be taking Lindsay to meet with AC to begin the search for his brother.

"Shit," Xav muttered.

He smiled tightly at a young woman whose gaze of admiration turned skeptical at his word and stomped past her toward the parking lot.

No cup of hot coffee in the warm lodge for him today. Xav stowed his gear in the SUV he'd switched to for mountain driving and headed down the road as fast as he dared, making straight for the offices of DX Security.

———

DIEGO INSISTED ON DRIVING LINDSAY FROM SHIFTERTOWN TO DX's offices, and Lindsay acquiesced. In spite of her self-confidence about this mission, she didn't trust AC at all and figured sticking close to Diego would be prudent.

She waited for him to pick her up as the evening deepened, after a day of trying not to think about Xav's perfect back as he'd walked away from her. Was it really over? The camaraderie, the stolen kisses, the joy of simply being in Xav's presence?

Lindsay hadn't tried to persuade him back to her, had she? She wondered if some part of her knew she'd never form the mate bond with Xav, and so had let him go.

The tightness in her chest, which flared up off and on, seemed to confirm her fears.

Diego arrived punctually, as Diego always did. Lindsay climbed into the front seat of the SUV, and then Diego raised his brows when the Shiftertown Guardian, Neal Ingram, complete with broadsword, slid into the back.

"I didn't want to come without Shifter backup," Lindsay replied to Diego's silent question. "Your teams are well and good, but I want a Shifter at my side. Neal can scare people just by looking at them, and he didn't have any other plans."

"No souls to send to the Summerland tonight," Neal said with dark humor.

Neal was a Lupine, and kind of a loner, as most Guardians were. The Sword of the Guardian wasn't simply a weapon—when a Shifter passed away, the Guardian released his or her soul to the afterlife by plunging the sword into the Shifter's heart. A soul not freed was liable to be captured by Fae mages who could trap and torment them for the enjoyment of it.

Also, the sword was sharp and painful when stuck into the living.

"Sure you want to get into this?" Diego asked, regarding Neal through the rearview mirror.

"I'm sure Eric wants me to bring Lindsay home alive or face his wrath." Neal shrugged. "It's no trouble."

No one in the car bothered to wonder why neither Diego nor Lindsay had asked Cassidy along. Diego would never risk her, Lindsay knew, though she'd bet he and Cassidy'd had an argument about it, similar to the ones she'd had with Xav.

The difference was that Diego would go home to Cassidy and they'd make up, probably with amazing sex, while Lindsay would retire to bed, alone and hurting.

They made the drive to DX Security in silence, neither man mercifully asking Lindsay why Xav wasn't with her. Neal had sensed something was up when Lindsay had called him to invite him along, and he kept tactfully quiet. Diego likely already knew the story, and he said nothing as well.

Diego kept his eyes on the road, and Neal, holding the sword across his lap so it wouldn't be visible to passing vehicles, pretended to be interested in the darkening streets.

Lindsay wished she wouldn't keep picturing Xav walking off in his usual efficient stride. She'd wanted him to turn back around, laugh his velvet laugh, and tell her he couldn't ever stay mad at her.

But he hadn't. Lindsay had hidden herself behind a convenient creosote, shucked her clothes, shifted, and gone for a long run. It hadn't tired her out or rid her of her heartache, only put stickers in her fur and got her chased by a loose dog.

When they arrived at DX Security, AC was already in an interview room, guarded by one of Diego's men, his hands bound once more.

AC had agreed to stay in a holding cell at DX Security, Diego said—it was either that or the nearest jail. Diego hadn't promised to *not* cart AC to the police after they found Dean, but he was being nice for now. It wasn't AC's brother's fault that AC was a dickhead, Lindsay imagined was Diego's reasoning.

AC watched Diego enter without belligerence, as though this was all going the way he wanted it to.

Diego had requested that Lindsay view the meeting through the glass in the next room, and she agreed. She'd waste time with an argument, and Diego would get his way in the end anyway.

Neal watched beside her—Diego probably worried that Neal's scariness and big sword might make AC pass out or something.

"So." Diego's voice came through the speaker when everyone was settled. "Where do we start?"

"Out near the rifle and pistol range," AC answered without hesitation. "Like I said, that's where Dean *was*. I don't expect to find much, but the Shifter woman might be able to get a bead on him."

Diego shrugged. "You might be right."

"So, is she here?" AC demanded. "Are we going now?"

"Sure." Diego nodded to his guys, who surrounded AC while he got to his feet. "Time to move."

The men and Diego escorted AC into the hall, where Lindsay and Neal joined them.

"I showed up, don't worry," Lindsay said to AC. She tapped her nose. "Sniffer ready to go."

AC didn't look impressed. Neal gave him his impassive wolf stare, and AC grew a bit more nervous. "Who the hell is that?" he asked.

"This is Neal." Lindsay indicated the Lupine. "He's *my* backup."

"Yeah? What happened to your boyfriend?"

Lindsay didn't know how to answer, especially when the

DX guys who worked with Xav every day showed interest in the question.

She was spared thinking of a response by a voice that washed giddy relief over her.

"If you're talking about me, I'm right here." Xav stepped out of his office down the hall and waited for them. "Let's do this."

CHAPTER SEVEN

L indsay didn't have a chance to ask Xav why he'd suddenly appeared, because Diego hustled them all out the door, and she got directed into a different vehicle from him.

The three DX Security men Lindsay rode with were good guys—she'd met their wives and kids—but Lindsay really wanted to be side-by-side with Xav. She wouldn't be able to interrogate him in front of the others, but she could at least enjoy his closeness.

She made herself acknowledge that Xav hadn't come for *her* sake. He'd probably decided to help Diego, doing his job. Even so, Lindsay kept her gaze longingly on the SUV ahead of her, wishing she could be in it and near Xav, even if he didn't speak to her.

Traffic thinned as the convoy drove through less densely inhabited areas, until finally the SUV's headed into empty darkness. The shooting range AC referred to was a few miles past the outskirts of town, closed now under the wintery night sky.

The lead SUV that Diego drove continued past the range a few hundred yards then turned onto a dirt road that led into the desert. Not long later, Diego pulled to the edge of this road and halted.

The other vehicles eased in behind them. Lindsay hopped out once they stopped, glad she'd worn thick boots and a jacket. The fine day had become a cold night, the wind sharp.

She tried not to look at Xav as she joined the others. Xav studiously avoided glancing at Lindsay as well, but she knew he was aware of her exact whereabouts.

Neal closed in next to Lindsay, while Diego's men surrounded the still-bound AC.

Once AC indicated the direction they were to go, Diego signaled for them to start off. Lindsay marched behind a contingent of security men, with Neal and Xav bringing up the rear. She knew this placed her protectively in the middle of the pack, but she let them do so, for now.

They followed a faint trail that headed toward a low mountain range to the east of the road. Lindsay's boots ground on fine gravel of the desert floor, and she pulled her jacket closer as the wind strengthened.

She began to scent the presence of humans as they went on. By Neal's quiet growls, he could as well.

The scent was old, though. No one was out here but their little group and a few coyotes, puzzled by the nocturnal intrusion.

"Here." AC halted when they reached the foothills of a craggy mountain and gestured at a depression in the ground.

Mountains in this range were knifelike ridges that rose more or less straight from the desert floor. Rocky folds hugged their base—they stood in one of those folds now—and from there, the mountain soared upward. It would be a steep scramble to the top even for those who enjoyed rock climbing.

Neither Xav nor Diego would allow any of their guys to dive into a hole in the ground, though it appeared to be a natural cave, not a mine shaft. Lindsay recalled what Xav had warned her about AC tossing her inside to see if it was dangerous, and she shivered.

If the hole truly *was* part of a mine, it could drop a long way. People had sunk shafts in myriad places across this area in days gone by, seeking silver, gold, copper, and other minerals that might turn a profit. Most mines had been abandoned but few had been filled in or even boarded over.

Diego ordered his men to lower lanterns on ropes into the cave, and Xav, in charge of gadgets as usual, sent in a surveillance camera.

Lindsay dared move close enough to peer over Xav's shoulder at his tablet's screen. The images from the camera showed jagged walls that glittered with granite and quartz, but no sign of human presence—no discarded cans or bottles, tent stakes or cables. No critters, either, which was odd. Rabbits, gophers, or snakes might like this hidden space to hole up in. But maybe they didn't like the lingering smell of humans either.

Xav glanced at Lindsay as she leaned closer, and her body instantly heated. "I need to know what I'm getting into," she said to explain why she was at his elbow.

"She doesn't have to go all the way inside," AC stated. "I just need her to find my brother's scent."

"Why did they bring him here?" Xav asked him. "Why drag your brother all this way only to disappear with him again?"

"Hell if I know," AC snapped. "This was the intel I had, but when I checked it out, the place was already empty. That's why I wanted *her*."

Lindsay examined the image on Xav's screen, memorizing the layout of the cave. "I'm on it. Give me a sec."

She turned away to look for a big rock to hide behind, feeling the night grow even more cold the moment she left Xav's side.

Neal followed her for a few yards, then stopped and turned to face the others. He planted himself between the men and Lindsay, his sword glinting in warning.

Grateful, Lindsay ducked behind a boulder and quickly undressed, stuffing her clothes into the small bag she'd brought along. The cold was brutal against her bare skin, encouraging her to shift more quickly.

At least, she *wanted* to shift more quickly. Her wildcat had other ideas.

Lindsay stifled a yowl as her body slowly and painfully changed form, but finally she landed on four paws and shook out her fur.

The chill instantly receded, becoming nothing but a minor annoyance. Lindsay shoved her bag behind a rock with one paw and trotted out to rejoin the others.

AC stared in mild shock as she approached, as though he'd never seen a Shifter in animal form before. It was unnerving. Lindsay resisted the temptation to sit down and wash her whiskers, to see how he'd react.

Xav scowled at him, impatient to get on with it.

"I need the hat," AC said.

Lindsay blinked, wondering what the statement meant, but one of the DX guys pulled a baseball hat out of his pocket and handed it to AC, who took it awkwardly, his hands still bound.

AC showed it to Lindsay. "This is Dean's. I found it in his apartment. I hope his scent hasn't worn off since these guys confiscated it."

Diego's men would have searched AC, removing everything he had on him. Even a hat could become a weapon, or at least a distraction.

Lindsay rested on her haunches and gazed at AC impassively.

"I brought it so you could get a scent from it." AC spoke slowly and loudly, as though Lindsay had suddenly lost the ability to understand him. "You can track Dean from this, can't you?"

Lindsay intensified her stare. She had no intention of taking a nose-full of someone's stinky hat. She could smell the unwashed hair from here.

"She doesn't need to," Neal said. "All she needs is *your* scent."

AC looked puzzled. "Why?"

"Humans who share DNA have a similar scent," Neal explained. "You wouldn't notice, but we do. She can find Dean based on you."

AC frowned but tentatively stepped forward, offering his arm for a sniff. Lindsay backed off, wrinkling her nose. She could already smell him fine.

While AC growled, Lindsay moved a few steps into the depression in the ground and tested the air.

All these people around weren't helping. She picked up a lot of scents, Xav's most distracting of all.

His was smoky and dark, sexy and inviting. Lindsay wished they were alone, somewhere they could be themselves, without anger and frustration between them.

But a man might be in danger, and Lindsay couldn't in good conscience leave him to suffer when she could help.

The brother, Dean, had been here, that was certain. He and whoever had taken him had entered the cave for a bit, maybe to get out of the winter rain that had pounded the area a few days ago, but they hadn't stayed long. They'd climbed out again, leaving the strongest scents outside the cave, which was a relief. Lindsay wouldn't need to descend all the way into it.

Dean had been with five human men, though none had scents Lindsay recognized.

It would have been nice to pinpoint exactly who'd taken Dean and so have some lead on where they might have gone with him, but life rarely worked out so neatly.

Lindsay delicately sniffed the air again, separating scents, tucking them into precise compartments in her mind. The men and Dean had lingered here outside the cave—why, she couldn't say—and then they'd walked away.

Her nose told her they'd headed back to flatter ground. Lindsay followed the scent trail around the group of men who watched her and into the open, heading north. She knew that a small campground lay outside a wildlife refuge at the foot of the mountains in that direction. Worth checking out.

Xav and the others followed Lindsay cautiously as she proceeded, trying to ignore the sounds of them tramping after her.

Dean's group had moved toward the base of the mountain range from which Gass Peak poked six thousand and more feet into the sky. Good hiking, Lindsay had always heard, though she'd never been up there herself.

Lindsay wondered why they'd chosen to take Dean straight across the desert floor. The nearby highway offered a much easier to navigate route to the campground, while hiking across country brought many perils.

All kinds of hidden washes and sinkholes under thin-crusted soil could trap the unwary, or at the very least break an ankle. Getting stranded out here for any length of time could be deadly.

Maybe that's what Dean's captors had meant for him. To

leave him or his body here for the coyotes and buzzards to pick over.

Lindsay smelled no death on the air, however. She'd have noticed that right away.

She kept moving, easily avoiding the hazards that would trip humans, her paws cushioned against the sharp pebbles on the ground.

Xav caught up to her while the others trailed behind. He moved with near-Shifter agility, avoiding cracks in the earth or stray rocks that could induce a fall. He'd told Lindsay he'd been hiking this wilderness since he'd been a kid, and he'd know this world even better than she did.

Lindsay and her folks had lived in a Shiftertown in Nebraska after they'd been rounded up from their home in the northern Canada until about ten years ago. Then their Shiftertown had closed and consolidated, Shifter Bureau thinking nothing of breaking up friendships and ties between Shifters to relocate them.

The move to the Las Vegas Shiftertown had been hard on Lindsay. If it hadn't been for Cassidy and her family, she'd have despaired.

Now she had Xav on her mind, all day every day, to stir her mating frenzy. Inconvenient, because he'd just broken up with her.

Lindsay blinked moisture from her eyes—stupid dust—and continued.

The scent trail led her to the campground, remote, dark, and empty. No one had bothered to pitch a tent on this freezing cold winter night.

The group she tracked had been here. Lindsay easily picked up Dean's scent, stronger this time, meaning their stay here had been more recent. And he'd been worried.

Lindsay turned to Neal, trying to explain in body language what she'd found. He was Lupine, she Feline, and cross-species communication was difficult, but Neal got the gist.

So did Xav, surprisingly.

"He was here," Xav announced before Neal could speak. "Linds, do you know how many were with him?"

AC watched Lindsay intently, as though he expected her to pound out the number with her paw, like a trained horse.

Lindsay smothered a sigh, extended a claw, and traced out the number 5 in the loose dirt.

"Fuck." AC muttered. "I don't want to fight off five guys on my own." He switched his hard gaze to Xav.

Xav shook his head. "You hired us—no, you hired Lindsay —to track down your brother. If you want us to help you fight to free him, that's extra."

AC glared. "You really are a bastard, aren't you? I knew that when you and your brother hauled me off to jail before. No mercy."

"Oh, we have mercy." Xav sent him the smile that made villains wonder if he was truly a good guy or not. "But we're not sacrificing ourselves for you. We're helping you search because we feel sorry for your brother. No other reason."

Lindsay edged closer to Xav, signifying she agreed with him. Plus, she'd take any excuse to be next to him.

She reminded herself that he'd left her today. Implied it was over—whatever *this* was.

So why had he showed up tonight? To protect her? That's what Neal and Diego were for, not to mention the other security men. Xav had no real reason to come along.

The idea that Xav had wanted to make sure Diego and their employees didn't fail Lindsay brought a warm glow to her heart. She tried to banish the cozy feeling, but in her lynx form, complicated human emotions tended to fade, and straightforward ones took over.

Her Shifter self acknowledged that Xav was hot and that

he cared about her safety. It was enough. All the words just got in the way.

AC scanned the darkness. "So, where are they now?"

Lindsay made herself leave Xav's side and continue her circuit of the campsite. Dean and his captors had lingered here longer than they had at the cave, maybe even sleeping here, but why and where they'd gone after that was fuzzy.

She wandered past the campground, trying to ignore the lantern flashlights everyone but Neal carried, which impaired her night vision. She found more traces of scent, very faint, and followed them.

Lindsay again wondered why Dean's captors had come to this remote area. To meet someone? To pick up something left for them? To hand off Dean to another crew? They hadn't dumped him, or she'd have found him already.

She didn't smell anyone other than Dean and his captors in or beyond the campsite. No one had used this place since the weather had turned raw, so there were no confusing over-laying smells. From what she could tell, only Dean and the other men had been here recently.

She also couldn't pinpoint a scent trail that led away from here. She did smell oil and diesel, and concluded that a truck or some other vehicle had awaited the group and taken them away.

Lindsay trotted back to the circle of men and gazed up at Neal, hoping he understood her.

"Trail ends here," Neal announced. He too tested the wind. "I think they drove back to the highway."

AC balled his hands in frustration. "You *think*?" He switched his gaze to Lindsay. "Where did they go? Where are they, you useless bitch?"

He lunged at Lindsay and found himself staring down both a broadsword and a blunt, black taser. Neal and Xav had put themselves between Lindsay and AC. She contented herself with a warning growl.

"She's got to keep looking," AC all but shouted. "Make her go back out there. They must have taken my brother *somewhere*."

"We'll continue the search at the DX offices," Diego said calmly from somewhere behind Lindsay. "We can find out what kind of vehicles came to the campground in the last week or so, and which way they went."

"How?" AC demanded. "Damn you, my brother could already be dead."

He wasn't, Lindsay knew. At least he hadn't been when he'd left here.

"She says he's probably alive," Neal translated. "Shifters can't follow the scent of someone who's been taken away in a rapidly moving vehicle. Then we can only smell truck, and that smells like every other truck."

Most Shifters couldn't, Lindsay amended to herself. One Shifter, called Tiger, could distinguish between various vehicles and even track them. But then, he had uncanny abilities that no other Shifter did. Diego could always ask if Tiger was available to help, though Tiger would come only if he wanted to.

"You mean that's it?" AC was demanding. "They brought my brother to this campground in the middle of nowhere, but who the hell knows where he is now?" He pointed a blunt finger at Lindsay. "I'm not paying you for a whole lotta nothing."

Lindsay lost her temper. She sprang at AC before she could stop herself, but Xav got in her way.

Lindsay pulled the leap, not wanting to hurt Xav, and ended up landing hard. Dust puffed around her and made her want to cough.

"Not worth it, Linds," Xav said in a firm voice.

Lindsay had to do *something*. Her adrenaline was high, she was annoyed she'd lost Dean's trail, and she was enraged at AC for being such a shit. His poor brother was probably in trouble, and she could do nothing about it.

Her wildcat refused to stand still and calmly wait for Diego to give orders. Fighting frenzy was taking over.

She let out a yowling growl, vaulted past Xav, and ran into the desert darkness.

CHAPTER EIGHT

X av flashed his lantern into the darkness after the fast-moving cat. "Lindsay!" he called. "Wait! *Dios mio.*"

"She'll be all right," Neal said tightly. He still had the sword trained on AC, who eyed it warily. "Shifter lynxes were bred for this kind of terrain."

"It's not the terrain I'm worried about," Xav said tightly.

The darkness could hold other dangers, from drug dealer exchanges to people in weird cults. Even an innocuous camper could shoot Lindsay because they'd think it cool to bag a giant wildcat.

Without another word, Xav started off after her.

"Want backup?" one of the DX men offered.

"I'll shout if I need it," Xav said without turning. Everyone had walkies if phones didn't work, and Diego had put a new tracker on Xav. Big brother wasn't risking losing little brother a second time.

Xav figured Lindsay was working off steam, like he'd done with his impromptu ski trip today. He also knew Neal was right—she'd probably be fine. But Xav couldn't stop himself tramping out into the darkness, his heart hammering.

His flashlight soon picked her up. Lindsay was loping along, moving fast but not fleeing. Xav jogged toward her, choosing his footing carefully.

Moonlight caught Lindsay's pale fur as she climbed a rise. She wasn't hiding, which was good, because Xav knew he'd never find her if she didn't want him to.

Lindsay finally halted halfway up the slope, putting a rock-strewn ridge between her and the view of the men gathered at the campground.

Xav's breath came fast as he climbed the hill, and he collapsed onto a boulder next to where Lindsay waited.

"AC's an asshole, Linds," Xav said to the silent cat who sank down next to him. "Always was. But he'll pay you what he owes you. I'll make sure of it. He'll also be grateful for your help. I'll make sure of that too."

Lindsay turned green eyes on him that held Feline skepticism. Xav couldn't read her body language like Shifters could, but he quickly understood. She was sick of humans—all of them.

Xav switched off the flashlight and gazed across the pristine landscape, this area isolated by the protected wilderness around them. The slice of moon brushed the rocks with silver light and glittered on quartz-laden gravel. Stars smeared the sky, the lights of Las Vegas obscured enough to render dimmer constellations visible.

"Nice night," Xav said. The wind picked up again, and he shivered. "Cold, though."

In silence, Lindsay rose and moved closer to him, sinking down with her side pressed along his right leg. Her body warmth stole over him, making Xav want to rub his hands through her fur.

He resisted, not wanting her to snarl and leap away. It was nice to have her close.

"I know you're concerned about Dean," Xav said. "So am

I." He drew his left foot up onto the boulder to stretch his knee. "We'll find him."

Lindsay huffed, her breath fogging in the cold air. Xav wished she'd talk to him, but she probably didn't want to become human while her clothes were stashed back at the cave.

"Wanna go for a beer after?" Xav suggested. "It's still early."

Lindsay's impassive gaze didn't give him an answer one way or the other.

He'd been in a very bad mood when he'd walked away from her earlier today. Xav wouldn't blame her for telling him to jump off a cliff and take his condescending attitude with him.

There were plenty of cliffs around here, in fact. If Lindsay shifted into her half-Shifter, half-human form, she'd be strong enough to drag him to one and drop him over.

Xav pulled his gaze from the nearest sharp ridge to find Lindsay gone, the cold by his side even greater than before. He stood up quickly, but to his relief saw her picking her way down the far side of the hill.

Xav switched on his flashlight and went after her.

Instead of running in frustration, Lindsay moved with deliberation, as though heading for a specific spot. Xav slipped and slid on gravel as he descended the rise, but he made it to the bottom without mishap.

Lindsay trotted onto a very flat, dry lakebed whose water had evaporated centuries ago. The depression might fill an inch when torrential rains poured down the mountain's washes, but now, despite the rain a few days ago, it was completely arid.

Xav caught up to Lindsay as she halted, her nose twitching, and stared with intensity at the middle of the lake bed.

Xav clicked off his light and stood with her for some time, letting the moonlight take over.

He didn't need night vision goggles to make out what Lindsay had spotted. In the middle of the lake bed, the dust had been disturbed by something that had blown it into widening, concentric circles.

Lindsay looked up at him with a glint of triumph in her eyes.

Xav walked toward the markings, Lindsay padding beside him. In the middle of the dust circles, he found the unmistakable signs of what he'd suspected he would.

He smelled nothing, because a good ground crew would make certain no oil or other fluid leaked, but Lindsay, with her superior senses had likely detected the exhaust.

"They took him out in a helicopter," Xav said softly. "Good one, Linds."

Lindsay huffed, as though happy he'd caught on.

Xav grinned down at her. "Helicopters can fly anywhere, sure, but air traffic is hard to hide. I'd say this really does call for a beer."

Lindsay didn't respond. She turned her back and walked away again, heading down a path he couldn't see that led in more or less the direction of the campground.

Without question, Xav followed her.

———

LINDSAY DRESSED IN THE SHELTER OF THE BOULDERS BACK AT the cave with both Neal and Xav ensuring that attention didn't focus on her. She grabbed her bag and joined the others, uncertainty making her legs wobble. Or maybe it was the agony of shifting after long treks on uneven terrain.

As she neared Xav, her whole body gave a throb. Nope, uncertainty.

AC was busily insisting that DX Security have Lindsay sniff out wherever the helicopter had gone, *right now*. Idiot.

"We have the means of finding it," Xav said coldly. "You sit tight and let us do our jobs. If your brother is being held against his will, we'll do everything to get him back."

"Sit tight, where?" AC demanded. "I'm not rotting in your little do-it-yourself cell. If you want to have me arrested for detaining your brother, go ahead, or else I'm out of here. You can't hold me against *my* will."

"You're not calling the shots," Diego informed him. "But no, you won't have to stay in our cell. We don't have the resources for long-term guests."

AC relaxed. "Fine, then you can drop me off at my apartment in Henderson. I won't be going anywhere until we find Dean."

Diego fixed him with his steely gaze. "I have another place in mind. It's not far, but it's cozy, with plenty of food." He turned to Xav. "You want to do the honors?"

Lindsay watched Xav stiffen. "I'm too busy to babysit tonight, bro."

Diego gazed at Xav for a long time, and Xav met his stare without flinching. Lindsay watched something pass between them, communication among brothers only they could read.

Diego finally gave Xav a nod. "All right. Neal?"

Neal adjusted the sword on his back. "Sure."

AC's eyes widened. "You can't cart me off with Shifters—that's in violation of so many laws. I'll have Shifter Bureau down on your ass so fast you won't know what hit you."

"I always love it when criminals threaten me with the law." Diego sounded amused. "Don't worry, the place I'm sending you is owned by a human and a long way from Shiftertown. Neal will accompany us and patrol the perimeter. For your protection."

AC didn't look convinced, but with armed guards who

clearly didn't like him surrounding him, his only choice was to capitulate.

Xav turned away as Diego gave orders as to who would do what. "Let's go," he said quietly to Lindsay.

Lindsay didn't argue. She followed Xav back down the trail from the cave to the waiting vehicles and climbed into his SUV. She was too distracted to wonder if there'd be enough room for the others in the remaining vehicles. Probably there would be—Xav wouldn't drive off otherwise.

They didn't speak as Xav moved slowly along the rutted road to the highway and then turned onto smooth, empty pavement. Xav didn't mention the celebratory beer again, only drove toward Las Vegas without any suggestion of a stop.

The sky had grown darker, with the moon already setting and very little traffic this far outside of town on a winter night.

Xav finally broke the silence. "He's taking AC up to Iona's cabin."

Iona's mother owned a cabin on Mount Charleston that she generously lent to Shifters. It was a nice retreat from the heat of summer and great for a run in the deep woods when Shiftertown grew too confining. Lindsay sometimes went up with Cassidy, Diego, and Amanda, which was more fun when Xav came along.

The cabin was difficult to reach on snowy days, a good place to isolate oneself, or to stash a villain in that Diego wanted to keep track of.

"I figured," Lindsay answered. "Why didn't you want to go?"

Xav shook his head. "I've spent way too much time with that guy already. Diego has plenty of competent people to help him out. I need a night off."

"You said you were too busy to watch him." Lindsay couldn't stop her need to know. "Busy doing what?"

Xav shrugged. "Stuff."

When Xav didn't want to answer, twenty feral Shifters couldn't pry information from him.

"Okay." Lindsay strove to sound nonchalant. "Well, thanks for not volunteering *me* to babysit."

Xav's jaw tightened. "I don't want AC anywhere near you. I'm happy Neal has his sword."

AC seemed more afraid of the Sword of the Guardian than all the firearms and tasers Diego's guys carried. Wise of him.

"Neal can take care of himself," Lindsay answered, for something to say. "You don't have to drive me all the way home. Drop me off at Shiftertown's gates, and I'll walk from there."

Xav glanced at the bag at Lindsay's feet. "You don't have a party dress in there? You're not going to run off to a club?"

"Not tonight. I'm tired. It's a cup-of-hot-chocolate-and-a-good-book night. Though I might pop in to see Cassidy, tell her what happened. She must be itching to know."

"I think she'll grill Diego just fine," Xav said with a touch of humor.

"I can soften things for Diego if she's prepped." Lindsay shared a smile with him.

It felt good to connect over their mutual understanding of Cassidy and Diego, but would it last? Or were they destined to be just friends from now on, maybe downgrading in time to mere acquaintances?

Xav grew quiet again, and Lindsay stared out the window, watching the starlit hills roll by.

She was intrigued about how Xav thought he'd track a helicopter, but she felt awkward asking—or saying anything at all. Of course, Xav could find things on a computer like no one else. Even Neal stood in awe of Xav's cyber skills.

Guardians were among the world's greatest hackers, so Neal's praise was huge.

Not long later, Xav pulled down the side road that took them to Shiftertown. He braked outside the gates but only to drive over the bump in the pavement that demarcated Shiftertown's entrance before he continued inside.

Lindsay gazed at him in surprise. "I said you could drop me off."

Xav didn't stop. "A gentleman doesn't let his lady walk home alone in the dark."

"I'm a Shifter." Lindsay let out a laugh, even as her heart pounded. *His lady?*

"Doesn't matter."

Xav slowly navigated the narrow streets in silence. Callum's birthday party was long over, but since many Shifters were nocturnal, cubs and their parents were still out prowling in wildcat or wolf form. Only the bears liked to turn in early.

Shifters they passed recognized Xav's SUV and either waved or let out growls of greeting. Xav politely returned the waves with a lift of his hand, then he pulled to a halt outside Lindsay's house and turned off the engine.

"Want to come in?" Lindsay asked, though not as enthusiastically as she usually would. She wasn't certain she could sit through polite chatter between Xav and her parents while she tried to decide her relationship status with him.

"No." Xav stared straight through the front window. "I think I should go home."

Lindsay fought disappointment. Having him converse with her parents while she stewed was better than not having him there at all.

"Okay, then." Her statement was soft. "I guess I'll say good night."

She touched the door handle.

"Lindsay."

Lindsay let go of the handle so fast it burned her fingers. "What?"

Xav turned in his seat to face her. "Just ..."

Lindsay expected him to start in again about her taking AC's offer, or for running off into the wilderness when her frustration wouldn't let her stand still, or for ... whatever he could think of.

Instead, he sat mutely, while Lindsay's heart raced.

"Good night, Xav," she said with more finality after a few moments had gone by.

Xav's jacket rustled as he moved to her. Before Lindsay could reach for the door handle again, Xav seized her face between his strong hands, stilling her, and kissed her firmly on the mouth.

CHAPTER NINE

The kiss was demanding, Xav's hands on her face unyielding. Lindsay rose to return it with a vigorous one of her own, while emotions tore through her and made her shake.

Xav had never kissed her like this before. Possessive, searing, holding her as though he feared she'd yank herself away and flee, never to seek him again.

Lindsay hooked her fingers around the lapels of his jacket and pulled him closer.

She was hot all the way through, her mating need flaring with a vengeance. Xav had to let her go, shove her out of the car, drive away. Or else Lindsay would be all over him, not caring what Shifters wandered by to peer through the quickly fogging windows.

Instead, Xav kept kissing her, drawing her up to him as his mouth commanded hers. Lindsay surrendered, the Shifter in her purring in satisfaction.

When Xav at last eased the kiss to a close, he held her with eyes dark as the night. His breath came fast, as did hers.

"Still want me to come in?" he whispered.

Come in. Yes, into me. To have me in the way the Goddess meant for us to be.

"No," Lindsay whispered back.

"Want me to go?"

Lindsay closed her hands more tightly on his thick jacket. "No."

Xav's grin was feral. He gently disentangled her from his coat, started the SUV, and pulled away from the curb.

Lindsay felt, rather than saw, her mom and dad at the front window, watching them go.

———

THERE WAS ONLY ONE PLACE XAV COULD TAKE LINDSAY WHERE they could be completely alone. He drove out of Shiftertown and headed the short distance to his own house.

He'd moved into the place near Sunrise Mountain not long ago, wanting something larger and more permanent than the apartment he'd been living in. DX Security was doing well, and Xav had decided the time was right for his own home.

He was glad he'd made the choice, because now he had someplace private, far from the prying eyes of Shifters and too-close neighbors.

Xav pulled the SUV into the garage beside his Mustang and turned off the vehicle. Lindsay didn't move. She hadn't spoken at all since they'd left Shiftertown.

When Xav clicked the switch to lower the garage door, Lindsay finally looked at him. "Are Shifters allowed in this neighborhood?"

Xav forced a smile. "Of course they are. It's why I bought the house. Besides, I really don't care what my neighbors think of my houseguests."

"You should. Shifter Bureau can be relentless."

"I'm Latino," Xav returned. "My neighbors didn't faint from horror about that, and most of them have been pretty friendly. Anyway, when did you become so concerned about what Shifters are or aren't allowed to do?"

"Since you brought me to your *house*. It's different."

Xav wasn't certain how it was different, but he didn't argue. He didn't want her jumping out and racing off to grab a cab home because he decided to quibble.

"I like showing off the place." Xav popped open his door and slid out. "Come on."

They hadn't mentioned the kiss, and now Xav felt awkward about it. Which was weird, because they'd kissed plenty before. They'd kissed, they'd danced, they'd played— they'd done everything but talk about important things.

This last seemed to be against Lindsay's rulebook, and Xav hadn't pushed her, pretending he didn't care one way or another. He simply sat back and enjoyed being with her.

Lately he'd started wanting something more than their back and forth, but maybe that was something Lindsay wasn't ready to give to him.

To Xav's relief, Lindsay hopped out of the SUV and followed him to the back door. He unlocked it and pushed it open, ushering Lindsay inside. He knew Shifter men entered houses first, in case danger awaited, but *his* rules of courtesy, drilled into him by his mother since he could talk, took over. Lindsay only stepped inside, as though she didn't mind, and waited for him to shut the door.

Xav led her into the kitchen, which boasted the latest fancy appliances, where he could cook and bake when stress got too much for him. He wasn't as good a cook as Diego or Mamita, but Xav could hold his own.

"Want coffee?" Xav offered. "Or wine? Beer? Milk?"

Lindsay, who'd been wandering through the kitchen,

swung around, her brows climbing. "Milk? Because I'm a cat?"

"No, because it's all I have in my refrigerator." Xav gestured to the door he'd opened. "Milk, water, beer, chilled wine. What will it be?"

Lindsay softened into a faint smile. "Wine, please. Doesn't have to be cold."

Xav obliged with a chardonnay he'd been saving for a special occasion. Lindsay coming over definitely counted as a special occasion.

He chose a red for himself, and they clinked glasses before drinking.

These uncomfortable silences between them were new. Xav had always been able to flirt and laugh with Lindsay without inhibition, but tonight he was tongue-tied.

He realized with a jolt that he'd been voluble so they'd never have to speak about anything serious. In these past few days, things had grown more serious than he could handle.

They drank more wine, both leaning against the kitchen counter. Not the most romantic spot, but neither seemed to want to move.

Xav cleared his throat. "Should we take this slow?"

Lindsay smiled, and his heart turned inside out. "No."

Xav set aside his wine and went to her. Lindsay clicked her wine glass down next to his and wrapped her arms around him.

Their first kiss was unhurried, in spite of Lindsay's words, as though they were getting acquainted. Xav slid fingers through her golden hair, which was gloriously thick and soft, letting it spill over his hands.

She tasted of the cool wine and a spice that was all her own. Xav pulled her closer, his body thrumming at the touch of hers against it. Lindsay was all sexy curves, but she had strength that no other woman in his experience possessed.

The shyness they'd both retreated into in the car began to drop away. Lindsay held on tighter, her kiss turning frenzied.

To hell with it. Xav wanted her, she wanted him, and there was only one reason they'd come to this house. It wasn't as though they hadn't played before, even if Lindsay had backed off wanting to complete things.

Xav slid his hands beneath the light sweatshirt she'd donned for tonight's adventure. Her skin was hot beneath it, the scalding temperature only a Shifter's body could reach.

Lindsay helped him skim the shirt off over her head, and she dropped it to the countertop. Xav lifted her there, stepping between her thighs to continue to kiss her.

Her bra came off next, Xav having in the past learned the intricate hooks of her lingerie. Lindsay was an athletic woman when she needed to be, but she also liked tiny bits of satin next to her skin. Xav didn't mind at all.

Lindsay held onto him as she kissed him, her earlier hesitance vanishing. Xav caressed her bare skin, bringing his hands up to cup her full breasts.

There was nothing small about Lindsay. She was a wonderful handful, and she was even better in his mouth.

Lindsay groaned as Xav savored her, tracing her velvety nipple with his tongue, suckling her softly. She cradled his head in her hands, furrowing his hair.

"Xav." Her hoarse whisper made Xav—reluctantly—release her. He licked her nipple one last time then raised his head.

"You okay, Linds?"

Lindsay rubbed the base of his neck. "I need ..." She went silent, desperation in her eyes.

Xav's breath came faster. "I know. I need it too."

"Good."

Lindsay launched herself at him. Xav caught her in his arms, right where he wanted her to be.

They savored each other, hands roving, mouths seeking. Xav heard his sweatshirt tear, and then pieces of it fell to the floor. He wore a long-sleeved T-shirt underneath, layers for warmth. That too, became shreds.

Lindsay slanted a smile at him, the claws she'd sprouted receding.

Xav didn't mind her bare breasts against his equally bare chest, their heartbeats speeding together. He kissed her mouth, chin, throat, then moved to her shoulder, which he nipped. He felt her teeth along his neck and laughed when she suckled.

The next thing he knew, his belt was open, his jeans unzipped, the fabric sagging down his thighs.

Two could play at that game. Xav popped open the button of the pants Lindsay had donned for the quest, and she wriggled herself free of them.

If they didn't get to the bedroom soon, they were going to do this standing up in the kitchen. Which wouldn't be a bad thing, the dim part of Xav's mind reflected.

Lindsay wriggled again, her last layers of clothing falling away. She tucked her hands under the waistband of Xav's underwear, and then that was shredded too.

They faced each other, breathing hard, Lindsay's eyes holding both questions and need.

Xav's body flamed, his heart pumping furiously. He was hard, wanting her, drinking in her beauty.

No time for the bedroom. Lindsay let out a squeal of delight as Xav lifted her to the counter once more. He stepped between her legs, scooted her to the edge, and positioned his cock directly at her opening.

"Yes?" he whispered. He shook all over, hoping like hell she didn't reject him, but if she did, he'd be a gentleman about it. It would kill him, but he'd do it.

"Goddess." Lindsay's word held vast longing. "Yes, Xav. *Please.*"

Xav groaned and thrust himself home.

———

LINDSAY'S WORLD CHANGED AS SHE AND XAV BECAME ONE. *THIS* is what she'd been craving since she'd first seen him, though she hadn't understood it.

A good-looking man she thought would be fun, she'd decided. But fun wasn't enough. Lindsay needed more and more. All of him.

She had all of him inside her now, Lindsay mused as her ecstasy soared. She rocked back on the counter, bracing herself with hands on his shoulders, taking him as far as she could.

Xav made a raw noise as he thrust into her, his strong hands keeping her from falling. He was big, hard, opening her in an exquisite way. Joy rushed through her every limb, heat rippling, changing her into a being of blissful flame.

He was beautiful and he felt good. He was Lindsay's, not only for tonight but for always.

Her love. Her *mate.*

Xav might not think of himself as a mate—he was human, and they didn't always comprehend Shifter terms. But it didn't matter.

Xav had a connection to Lindsay, which her wildcat knew, deep inside herself.

Mate. *Mine.*

Lindsay drew him down to her as much as she could without jeopardizing their wonderful connection. Xav shuddered at he drove into her, sweat trickling, but his gaze was fixed on Lindsay, his eyes filled with liquid fire.

Lindsay kissed his throat where she'd left her love bite

and breathed her warm breath across his skin. Marking him. Hers.

Xav thrust faster, creating lightning heat inside her. Lindsay lifted herself to him, her legs tight around him. They were one, mates, fitting together perfectly. Exactly right.

She heard her own voice shrieking her delight, and Xav's groans answering. He shuddered once more, his hot seed finding its way home.

In that moment, Lindsay was complete. Her restlessness, her impetuous risks, her *need* for something she didn't understand was suddenly sated.

And would be, as long as she could be in Xav's arms.

Xav slowly but inexorably withdrew, and Lindsay reached for him, not wanting this to end.

"Lindsay." Xav gathered her to him, his smile as fierce as any Shifter's in mating frenzy. "Damn."

Lindsay couldn't speak. She tried to catch her breath, elated but nowhere near sated. She needed more, and more.

She started to wrap herself around Xav again, but he laughed and backed away. "Not here. Bedroom."

Before Lindsay could agree and race there, Xav swept her into his arms. He carried her out of the kitchen, across the living room, and down a hall into the last room at the end.

Xav's bedroom was large and a little cluttered, which was all Lindsay saw before Xav lowered her to the bed.

He stepped back to gaze at her with warm eyes, letting Lindsay take in his tall, strong body, his chest dusted with black curls, his thick cock ready once more. Lindsay bathed him in a wide smile then grabbed him by the hands and pulled him onto the bed. Xav, laughing, came to her.

This time as they fit together, Xav pressing her into the mattress, the spark in Lindsay's heart began to glow. She ignored it in the madness, twining her legs around him to pull him closer, but when things slowed, the glow strengthened.

After the third time they made love, Lindsay ended up on top of Xav, straddling him while Xav smiled at her with languid need.

The glow inside her became a solid warmth, spreading through Lindsay and scaring the shit out of her. When her current frenzy ended, she'd have to examine what it meant and how it would break her heart.

For now, she enjoyed Xav. Lindsay laughed with him as she took him inside her as far as she could.

They were one. Connected. And if her Shifter cat had her way, they'd stay that way for always.

———

Hours later, Lindsay lay on her side, watching Xav sleep. He'd crashed after he'd come inside her the last time, falling into profound slumber.

Lindsay was too exhilarated to relax.

She touched her chest, feeling her heart pounding, and wondered if she'd imagined the sensation that had seeped through her.

Nope, it was real.

Tendrils that Lindsay realized had been there for a while flared as she gazed at Xav. They'd tightened every time she'd seen him laugh, or whenever he'd taken her around a dance floor, or waved to her from Cassidy's house and jogged across the yard to see her.

It was in his smile, in his eyes, and now in Lindsay.

The mate bond.

The implications of that kept her awake as much as her adrenaline.

Xav was human. Lindsay knew humans *could* form the

mate bond, because she'd seen it in Diego and also in Misty for the impossible-to-love Graham.

But it was rare, and it couldn't be forced. If only one partner formed the bond, the one who didn't could walk away, unfazed.

If Xav did that, Lindsay would be left bereft, maybe for the rest of her life.

Mate bonds guaranteed that Shifter mates protected each other against the most dire of perils and also filled the world with cubs. It was an old magic, instilled in Shifters by the Goddess to ensure their survival, but that magic came with a price. The mate bond could tear as much as it tied.

Lindsay's parents shared the mate bond, a strong and sure one. It had carried them through the hardest times when they'd lived in different parts of northern Canada in the wild, through fear and sorrow, despair and resignation. Their love had endured, outlasting the moves to two Shiftertowns and the huge adjustments they'd had to make.

Lindsay had longed to find the mate bond, more possible now that they lived in a community, but even then, she'd thought herself destined to be alone.

Xavier Escobar had caught and held her attention the day she'd spied him with Diego at the ceremony honoring Cassidy's fallen mate—another drawback of the mate bond. The grief it caused was intense.

Lindsay had looked Xav over, and her heart had flopped around in a way that had confused her.

Hey, if I provide the handcuffs, do you think Diego's brother will do me the honor? Lindsay had said to Cassidy. She'd only been half joking.

Tonight had been better than that faraway day had promised. Lindsay had tried to keep things casual with Xav, being her teasing, never-be-nailed-down self, but that had been a facade.

Now, she was baring herself, in more ways than one.

Watching him sleep, Lindsay knew something had changed in her. She'd been running all her life, at first literally, when she and her parents had to do whatever they could to keep themselves alive.

Then evading Shifter Bureau, adjusting to life in two successive Shiftertowns, and now avoiding Graham's contentious Lupines while everyone in this Shiftertown figured out how to live together.

Lindsay was used to fleeing from anything too difficult, too scary. Lynxes were fast, built for speed, as they were small in the Shifter world, more vulnerable than the lions, leopards, and most especially the few, rare tigers. Lindsay knew that her friendship with Cassidy, Eric's second-in-command, held helped ease the Cummingses acceptance into the Las Vegas Shiftertown and kept the more powerful Felines from intimidating them.

When they'd lived in the wild, Lindsay's family had been ready to pick up and move at a moment's notice. Lindsay had always been happy to go, anticipating the next adventure.

Now, she wanted to stay.

She'd never have guessed her reason for sticking around was a human man with a velvety laugh and touch that drove her wild.

Xav's chest rose and fell evenly, he sleeping in deep relaxation. Lindsay was restless, wanting to go for a run or a hard hike in the mountains, or better still, have more sex with Xav.

He didn't look as though he'd be waking anytime soon, though. Lindsay decided to let him sleep—he needed the rest after their almost nonstop night. She wanted him ready for the next night, and the one after that.

Gray light was already peeking through the windows. Lindsay slid quietly from the bed, surprised that her muscles were a little sore, but then, some of the positions they'd tried ...

She shook herself, threw on a few garments from a pile on a chair, and made her way out to the kitchen.

Her folks probably guessed where she was—they'd seen Xav kiss Lindsay in the truck and then drive off with her. The windows of the SUV were darkened, but Shifter eyesight was keen.

She'd call them when it got lighter. Leah and Martin liked to sleep in on winter mornings, snuggled together, their mate bond wrapped around them. Without Lindsay in the house, they'd likely have felt the freedom to get caught up in a little mating frenzy of their own. She'd wait before disturbing them.

Lindsay retrieved the clothes they'd dropped to the kitchen floor, along with the tattered remains of Xav's sweatshirt and T-shirt. She laughed to herself, recalling how her impatient cat had shredded them to get to the man inside.

To her surprise, Lindsay heard the shower go on as she started the coffee maker. Xav must not have been as heavily asleep as she thought.

She considered hurrying back down the hall and jumping into the shower with him, but maybe he'd welcome a moment alone.

Or maybe Lindsay was too afraid to face what she felt for him. She wasn't certain anymore.

She took two cups out of the cupboard and glared at the coffee maker, willing it to hurry up. Shifters brewed in old-fashioned coffee pots on the stove, which were far less complicated to use. Xav had taught Lindsay about coffee makers, but she found she preferred stovetop pots, which had actually become trendy again with some humans.

The coffee maker's burbling sounds and the distant

pattering of the shower were interrupted by someone knocking firmly on the kitchen's back door.

Lindsay didn't hesitate to answer it. It might be Diego or a DX man with news, or it might be a neighbor, who'd need something important to come over this early.

The scent she caught wasn't Diego's, though it was familiar. Lindsay realized why when she flung open the door.

A black woman stood on the threshold, one in her thirties as humans counted years, with a perfect face, sleek hair drawn into a bun, and a lithe, athletic body. She wore a pink sweatshirt and gray leggings for running, and stared at Lindsay in surprise before she gave her a wide smile.

"Hello, Lindsay," Emma Shields said jovially. "Is Xav at home? I'm thinking he is, or else you wouldn't be here. Can I come in?"

CHAPTER TEN

After a moment of staring, all Lindsay could do was step back and allow Emma inside.

Emma headed into the kitchen as though she knew the exact layout of Xav's home. "That him in the shower?" she asked. "Ooh, coffee. Mind if I have some?"

Lindsay expected her to simply grab one of the two cups, but Emma politely waited for Lindsay to rummage around and produce another mug. The machine kept gurgling, emitting warm-smelling coffee, and Lindsay set the mug on the counter next to the others to wait.

"Kind of early for a visit." Lindsay's cat hackles were rising, her possessiveness too high. She needed to cool it.

The Shifter cat inside her wasn't listening. *My* mate. *Mine. Rowwwl.*

"I'm always up early," Emma said breezily. "I don't sleep much. Love a good run in the morning."

Her movements were as restless as Lindsay's. Lindsay's guard, which she'd let down to enjoy her time with Xav, rose high now that Emma, a woman Xav greatly admired, had zipped in, eager to see him.

"I know what you mean," Lindsay made herself say calmly.

I'm a cat, bitch. I can strike lightning fast, so watch out.

Emma gave Lindsay an assessing onceover. Lindsay had grabbed one of Xav's T-shirts, which hung past her hips, and wore nothing but her underwear she'd retrieved beneath it. She'd put on socks, because the floors were cold. She must look ridiculous.

Emma's smile became admiring. "Good for you, sweetie. He's been mooning over you too long. I bet you both needed that."

Lindsay felt herself blushing. She never blushed about sex. She was a Shifter, and Shifters had mating needs. Nothing to be embarrassed about.

She managed to shrug. "It was late. We were horny."

Emma burst out laughing. Even that sound was lovely.

"No judgement from me, honey. Xav is awesome, and he needs someone." She seemed to sense Lindsay's uneasiness, because she held up both hands. "Oh, not *me*. Unh-uh. I really like Xav, but we'd clash and crash. It would be a train wreck, without any fun to make it worthwhile."

The coffee maker beeped, signaling it was done. Lindsay distracted herself by pouring two cups and handing one to Emma.

"Why do you say that?" Lindsay asked, her curiosity pushing through her rancor. "About clashing and crashing? Xav and I clash too, but I don't mind."

"In a different way." Emma leaned comfortably against the counter and sipped her coffee. "You two were made to clash."

Lindsay didn't know what to make of that, so she took a gulp of coffee and didn't answer. Too confusing.

"I'm going to make an observation," Emma said, her gaze shrewd. "I've known Xav a while. Worked with him and

Diego on a number of jobs. Xav is sharp, can think on his feet. Never screws up a mission. But I only see him truly relax when he's with you, or when he's talking about you. Whatever magic you're working on him, it's a good thing."

Lindsay would love to think so. She wasn't relaxed at all when Xav's name came up. She either wanted to race around and yowl or be teasing and sarcastic.

"He also tries to tell me what to do," Lindsay couldn't stop herself saying. "I'm a cat, and cats don't like that. We love our independence."

Emma beamed her another big smile. "Well, you don't have to listen. Guys always think they have to shelter women, because back in caveman days, they kind of did. There must be a node in their brains that keeps telling them that. I've learned to nod and smile, and then do whatever the hell I want."

Lindsay found herself grinning in return. Maybe this woman she'd been so jealous of was more a kindred spirit.

"Shifter males *truly* have that node in their brains," Lindsay said. "They all believe I should mate with them, for my own protection, of course. They think it's weird that I like a human."

"They're feeling their biological clock ticking," Emma said. "They want cubs before they're old and decrepit. Don't look so surprised—I know a lot about Shifters. I once worked for Shifter Bureau."

The glimmer of camaraderie instantly died. Growls filled Lindsay's throat, and she felt her claws come. "Shifter Bureau?"

"Don't look at me like that. Back before I joined DX, I needed to do community service, and I got assigned to them. They're horrible. I always thought they wanted to do good— help Shifters integrate into society and make sure they get access to food and housing, and all that. But it's just another organization wanting to keep people who are different under their collective thumb. They offered me a permanent position when I was done, but I bailed. I learned a lot about Shifters in their databases, though, and later when I met people from your Shiftertown. Like Brody." She relaxed. "He's pretty cool."

At any other time, this interest in Brody might have piqued Lindsay's curiosity, but her suspicions were ramped high. "Xav and Diego must know you were with Shifter Bureau. And never bothered to tell me."

Emma's brows rose. "I'm surprised they mention me at all. I'm just another asset gathering data or helping on an extraction."

"No, they sing your praises. They say you're crazy smart and capable of handling very dangerous people."

"Really?" Emma continued to sound perplexed. "Hey, if I'm that amazing, I want a raise. Wait, is that why you looked at me like you wanted to scratch my eyes out when you opened the door?"

"Yes." Lindsay never saw any benefit in lying.

"Hm, well, I'm glad to hear Xav and Diego like me, but not that they're setting me up for grudges from people I have to work with. Or want to be friends with." She saluted Lindsay with her cup.

Lindsay started to soften again, though she'd told herself she'd remain cautious about a person who'd been trusted enough by Shifter Bureau to be offered a job. She lifted her cup in return. "Screw 'em. We'll be friends anyway."

Emma laughed. "I'll drink to that."

In this auspicious moment, Xav wandered into the kitchen. He was fully dressed—he must have heard that he had company—and was rubbing a towel over his very wet hair as he entered.

"Emma." He gave her a nod, went straight to Lindsay, cupped her hip, and kissed her on the mouth.

Lindsay gaped at him when he turned away, her lips tingling. Xav dumped the towel on a chair and headed for the coffee pot. Emma winked at Lindsay as he took up the remaining mug and filled it.

"I did some research on the names you and Diego gave me," Emma said as Xav turned, cup in hand. "I didn't want to talk about it over the phone, and I figured you'd be up by now for your run. I didn't realize you were busy." She smiled into her mug.

"No problem," Xav said. "What did you find out? You can talk in front of Lindsay. She's part of the team."

Lindsay warmed to his words, though *she'd* chosen this mission, so technically Xav was part of *her* team. But she wasn't going to fuss.

"AC Parkes, you know about," Emma began. "Busted by you and Diego for importing weapons to sell to gangs here and in L.A. He plea-bargained down, but still served about fifteen years." She peered at Xav. "You and Diego must have been babies when you arrested him."

"One of our first busts as detectives," Xav said without gloating. "Helped us move up the ranks."

"I'm sure. AC served out his time, kept his nose clean, took advantage of classes and work programs and emerged reformed, so his paperwork says. Ready to integrate back into society. *Dean* Parkes, his little brother—different story."

Xav settled in next to Lindsay, close enough that their arms touched. It was intimate, acknowledging that they belonged together.

Lindsay, so focused on the way the tendrils around her heart came to life, almost missed Emma's ongoing report.

"AC practically raised Dean, because their parents were in and out of rehab," Emma continued. "AC is nine years older than Dean. AC had a strict no-drug policy, because he saw what drugs did to their mom and dad. Dean pretty much stayed out of trouble until his brother went off to prison. He was fine at first while he finished up high school, but once Dean was out on his own, he started doing small jobs for gangs, then bigger jobs, and finally became tight with the leaders. He's been arrested a couple of times, but Dean seems smart. Evidence doesn't stick to him."

"Tallies with what AC told us about Dean falling in with some truly bad guys," Xav said. "So what happened? Did he piss off one of the higher-ups? Did they mean to kill him or not? Lindsay says Dean's most likely alive."

"He was when he got into the helicopter," Lindsay amended.

"Yeah, that's weird," Emma said. "What were they doing flying around in the middle of nowhere in a helicopter? Way to draw attention. If they took Dean to that area to kill him, why didn't they?"

"Maybe he talked his way out of it." Lindsay suggested. "That's what I'd do."

Xav chuckled. "Yeah, you'd be good at it. Better than I was with AC. He only kept me alive because he needed something."

Lindsay suppressed a shiver of disquiet. "The fact that we found you meant you did a pretty good job."

She recalled how she'd *known* that Xav had been taken the direction she'd decided to go, even without an obvious scent trail. She'd thought it had been Shifter instinct that led her across the desert to the old bank vault, but she wondered now if it had been the mate bond pulling at her.

The idea raised both hope and concern—Xav wouldn't necessarily form the bond with her in return. There was never any guarantee it would go both ways.

"How you can joke about being grabbed by a guy like Parkes is beyond me," Emma said. "I'd have shit myself."

"No, you'd have taken him out with your bare hands and

walked away," Xav said with continued good humor. "You wouldn't have let him get the drop on you at all. Even if you'd been seriously distracted, like I was at the time."

Emma shrugged. "Maybe."

Xav had been distracted by arguing with Lindsay for interfering with the mission to arrest the arms dealer. Xav might have been able to avoid AC's goons if she hadn't pissed him off, a thought that did not help her current agitation.

"Back to Dean," Xav said. "I'm guessing that he disagreed with his gang leaders for some reason. They decided to take him out to that campground, maybe planning to kill him, then changed their minds and left with him in a helicopter. A couple of the men with them probably drove away, which is why Lindsay and Neal smelled a vehicle of some kind at the campground. Helicopters only hold so many. We'll be working on where the helicopter went, flight paths, and so forth."

"That's up to you and your computer wizardry." Emma set down her empty cup. "I'm better with people."

"Which is why we send you out to ask questions," Xav said. "I have different help with the computers. In fact—here come some more early risers."

Xav gestured toward the kitchen window, which gave a view of a slice of front driveway. Two men had climbed out of a pickup that had pulled up to the house, one with a long, muffled object on his back. The other man was larger and wore a scowl.

"Wow, how'd you pry Brody out of bed at this hour?" Lindsay asked in surprise. "Looks like you'd better make more coffee."

"On it." Xav had another packet of coffee out of the nearest cupboard and more water in the coffee maker before Neal and Brody reached the back door. "Emma, can you let them in?"

Emma, who appeared suddenly uncertain, stepped to the door she'd so recently banged on and opened it as Neal raised his hand to knock.

Neal and Brody had both met Emma on previous DX Security missions, but they stopped and stared at her as though they'd never seen her before.

"We have the right house?" Brody growled behind Neal.

"This is the address he gave us," Neal said, his tone wary.

"Then what's she doing here?" Brody demanded.

Lindsay hurried to intervene, as Xav was working on the coffee and Emma had frozen, her hand on the doorknob.

"Way to say good morning," Lindsay told Neal and Brody. "Seriously rude, guys. Yes, Xav lives here. Yes, Emma is visiting. They work together, remember? I'm here for a different reason."

Brody's grumpy gaze softened the slightest bit. "Finally. If you two had kept apart any longer, I'd have lost a bet."

"Mind your own business, bear," Lindsay growled. "You can let them in now, Emma."

"Oh. Right." Emma jumped and swung the door wide, then quickly turned away before Neal and Brody stepped inside.

Neal unslung the wrapped broadsword from his back and stood it against the wall as Brody closed the door and lumbered into the kitchen in Emma's wake. Neal clicked the lock on the door, something he'd never do in Shiftertown, and sent Lindsay a silent glance.

His eyes abruptly narrowed—Guardians were more perceptive than other Shifters.

"Does he know?" Neal asked in a near whisper.

Lindsay's alarm sprang high, as did her elation. If Neal could sense the mate bond, maybe it was real. "No, and you aren't going to tell him."

Neal, a man of few words, stared hard at Lindsay and then went on into the kitchen.

"Coffee in a minute, Brody," Xav was saying. "You should have called ahead—I'd have had it fresh and hot."

"It *was* fresh and hot, but we drank it," Emma informed Brody. "You're too late."

Brody glared at her. "I was dragged out of bed at the crack of dawn on a *Monday* by a wolf with a sword. Now I'm being scolded by a human woman before I've had caffeine."

"Not scolding," Emma said with bravado. "Just stating the truth."

Brody stared back at her for a few moments, his dark eyes shielding his thoughts. "Whatever," he huffed and lumbered to the refrigerator, opening it to examine its contents.

"How's AC?" Xav asked Neal, ignoring the exchange.

"Surprisingly docile," Neal answered as he leaned comfortably against the counter. "Settled in at the cabin with no problem, went to bed, no sign of him trying to escape. Nell and Cormac relieved us so Brody could get his beauty sleep."

Brody backed out of the refrigerator with a pitcher of orange juice, scowling.

Xav chuckled. "Nell will keep AC in line." Brody's mom could be one mean grizzly. "Did you have time to track the info I wanted?" Xav continued to Neal. "Or did you need your beauty sleep too?"

"I have it." Neal regarded Xav impassively. "I'll need to get into the Guardian Network to show you, but that's no problem. I have my own hotspot."

"I have a VPN, if you're worried about anyone pinpointing your location," Xav answered.

Emma rolled her eyes. "And when they start with the nerd speak, I know it's time to leave."

"And me." Lindsay set her empty mug and Emma's in the

sink. "Can I bum a ride from you, Emma? You can let me off anywhere near Shiftertown."

Xav, who'd pulled a laptop out of the desk built into the end of his kitchen counter, set down the computer and moved swiftly to Lindsay. "You're going?"

Lindsay's heart fluttered as Xav laid a warm hand on her shoulder. "Watching you boys gaze at numbers on a screen isn't my idea of fun."

"Mine either," Brody broke in. "But Eric assigned me bodyguard duty. No choice."

Xav kept his focus on Lindsay. "I understand." He sounded deeply regretful, which spiked Lindsay's yearning higher. "When we're done here, mind if I come over?"

Lindsay was aware of the other three watching them intently, not even pretending they weren't eavesdropping.

"You'd better," Lindsay said softly. She smoothed her hand down Xav's chest. "How else am I going to know where to look for AC's brother?"

Xav touched his forehead to hers. "See you later, then."

"Guess so."

Xav cupped Lindsay's face with one hand and pulled her close for a kiss. Lindsay had meant to keep it short, because of their watchers, but one touch, and she was lost.

Xav tasted of coffee and afterglow, plus the tingling fire that confused Lindsay as much as it exhilarated her. The kiss turned deep, a spark of passion from the previous night igniting.

When they finally eased back, Lindsay realized she'd wrapped her arms all the way around Xav and pulled him close. She continued to hold him in the embrace Shifters used for comfort, for security, for the joy of being with that person.

Lindsay exhaled over Xav's neck, strengthening the scent mark she'd begun the night before.

Even now, Lindsay wasn't certain if Xav had escalated their relationship to one more serious but the scent mark broadcast to every Shifter that *she* had.

Xav sent her a puzzled look when Lindsay pulled away. "I'll call you when we're done," he promised.

"Sure," Lindsay said.

Xav's bewilderment grew as Lindsay quickly turned away. Neal and Brody stared at her hard, knowing exactly what she'd just done. Emma, sensing something was up, watched Neal and Brody.

"Let me get dressed and grab my stuff," Lindsay said to Emma. "Meet you out front."

Emma only nodded, and Lindsay left the kitchen as rapidly as she could. Brody watched her go in surprise that was turning to amusement, Neal in understanding.

———

"You gonna tell me what that was all about?" Emma asked as they headed out of Xav's neighborhood.

She drove a modest minivan, nothing flashy, which Lindsay supposed made sense if Emma wanted to keep herself low-key. No one paid attention to a thirty-something woman in a beige car.

Lindsay could have feigned innocence and said *What was what all about?* but she knew Emma would call bullshit.

"I marked Xav as mine."

Emma's brows rose. "You mean walking around in his T-shirt and not much else didn't say that loud and clear?"

Lindsay didn't laugh. "It's a Shifter thing. I thought you knew about Shifters."

"Apparently not everything. Subtleties can't be found in a database."

"Tell that to our male friends back at Xav's house."

Emma laughed. "I like you, Lindsay. I hope you don't mind. I'll take you all the way to Shiftertown, don't worry."

"I don't mind." It might be nice to have another friend. Lindsay still spent plenty of time with Cassidy, but it wasn't the same as when they'd run around everywhere together with no cares. Cassidy had a mate and cub now, with more to come, plus she had much to do being Eric's second.

Then again, Emma had been with Shifter Bureau. Lindsay didn't scent lies on her when Emma had proclaimed why she'd quit them, but it was wise to be cautious.

"Don't mind at all," Lindsay repeated. "Call me when you have a free night, and we'll party."

"Sounds good to me. Diego and his boys sure like to work."

"They do." Lindsay sighed. "Maybe a little too much."

"I saw the way Xav looked at you," Emma said as she navigated through Monday morning traffic. "And the way he kissed you. Trust me, Xavier's mind isn't entirely on his job."

Lindsay would like to think so. Her own thoughts, on the other hand, were all over the place. She needed a good run out in the open or through the mountain woods to sort things out.

It wasn't long before Emma turned down the long street that led to Shiftertown. Lindsay expected Emma to drop her off at the gates, but Emma continued through, as Xav had done last night.

Lindsay directed her to the Cummings house, and Emma slowed to a halt in front of it.

"I'm taking you up on the party thing," Emma informed Lindsay as Lindsay hopped out. "Hope you weren't just being polite, because I'm in the mood to dance."

Lindsay beamed her a smile. "Let's do it."

"I'll call you," Emma promised. "I have your number—Xav gave it to me for emergencies. See you, Lindsay."

Lindsay blinked at that information, but she sensed Emma impatient to get on with her day, so she stepped back with a quick good-bye. Emma lifted a hand as she pulled away, then she rounded the corner and was gone.

Lindsay sighed as she made her way into the house, rehearsing her explanation for being out all night, if necessary. Her parents were Shifters—they'd understand.

Her mother, in fact, intercepted Lindsay before she could dart down the hall to her bedroom.

"Lindsay, honey." Leah enfolded Lindsay in a motherly hug, holding her daughter close. Lindsay returned the embrace, sinking into the comfort her mom had given her all her life.

Leah eased away after a time but held Lindsay's shoulders as she gazed at her, Leah's eyes as green as Lindsay's own.

"I think we need to talk," Leah said. "Come on. Your dad wants to say something too."

Lindsay's alarm rose as her mother took her by the hand and led her deeper into the house.

CHAPTER ELEVEN

Leah took Lindsay not to the living room but opened the door behind the paneling in the hall that hid a staircase going down. Lindsay's uneasiness increased as they descended.

The staircase ended in a small space where another concealed door opened into a comfortable sitting area with a kitchenette. A large television, soft furniture, and lots of shelving with books and nicknacks made the place cozy.

Lindsay had spent much time in this basement when they'd first arrived in this Shiftertown, comforting herself with things she'd grown up with. Few of the other Shifters would believe that the outgoing and wild Lindsay had once been very shy.

Lindsay's father rose from a sofa, setting aside his coffee and newspaper.

"Sorry I didn't call," Lindsay said. She hadn't felt so nervous under her parents' gazes since she'd been in her Transition and worried them sick. "It was a spur-of-the-moment thing."

Martin shook his head. "Lindsay, you're a grown Shifter

and can come and go as you please. We knew you were with Xavier, and safe."

Bewilderment entered Lindsay's apprehension. "Then what's the problem? Why are we down here where no other Shifter will hear us?"

Leah slid her arm around her daughter. "Eric came to see us this morning."

Panic joined Lindsay's mix of emotions. "What happened? Is Cassidy okay? Is it the cub?"

"No, no, nothing like that." Leah squeezed Lindsay's waist, her touch instantly soothing. "Cassidy is fine and well, as are all of Eric's family. The subject was your mating."

Lindsay abruptly pulled away from her mother. "Seriously? Why is it anyone's business, especially Eric's? I have plenty of time to choose a mate, right? And no, I'm not picking one of Graham's annoying wolves."

The Lupines who'd been forcibly moved here from Graham's Shiftertown in northern Nevada had been clamoring for the single women of this Shiftertown to mate with them. The ladies had mostly refused.

Shifter Bureau had truly fucked over Graham and his Lupines, but that didn't mean Lindsay and every other unmated female would sacrifice themselves for them.

"Of course it's your choice," Martin said patiently. "But a couple of the Lupines are talking about Challenging Xavier for you. Eric came to warn us."

Lindsay's agitation sprang high again. "They can't Challenge him. Xav has never made a mate-claim. What are they talking about?"

A Challenge was basically trial by combat when another male Shifter wanted the female in question. It was usually only issued once a mate-claim had been formally made in the presence of witnesses.

"They believe the claim will come soon," Leah said. "You

staying with Xav last night will convince them they're right. They're trying to get rid of a rival before he's too entrenched. Eric says Graham's Lupines did such things when they lived in their former Shiftertown."

"Well, they don't live there now." Lindsay's heart banged, and she felt ill. Xav was no pushover, but a Challenge was traditionally to the death, and any human would lose in a direct fight with a Shifter. Plus, Graham's Lupines fought dirty.

"Graham is trying to make them see reason," Martin said. "He and Eric are on top of it—Eric doesn't want to see Xavier hurt either."

"What does Diego say about it?" Lindsay demanded.

Leah and Martin exchanged a glance. "Diego doesn't know," Martin said. "Eric wants to settle this quietly."

"Eric means he doesn't want Diego to go tase the Lupines until they puke," Lindsay said heatedly. "He doesn't want Graham to retaliate on Diego or Xav, which will put Eric at war with Graham. *Shit.*"

Lindsay turned and started for the door. Her wildcat wanted to scream, to bounce off walls and claw everyone who got in her way.

"Where are you going, Linds?" Her mother's gentle voice came behind her. "Do you need the cage?"

An hour banging around the room they'd constructed with padded walls and ledges they could leap between might help, but it wouldn't solve the bigger issue.

"I'm going to see Graham," Lindsay announced.

"No, Linds," Martin tried. "Leave it to Eric and Graham. They'll sort this out."

True, it was Eric's and Graham's jobs as leaders to cool their Shifters down and make sure no one got hurt.

The trouble was, Xav wasn't a Shifter. Would Graham really put himself out to keep Xav from harm? It was in

Graham's best interest for his Lupines to respect him, and defending a human against them wouldn't win Graham any points.

Lindsay headed out of the room, and her parents didn't stop her. She sensed them standing close together as she stormed up the stairs and into the main house again.

Once outside, Lindsay breathed a little easier, the cool winter breeze welcome.

Of course, all of Shiftertown would know that she'd spent the night with Xav. He'd kissed her pretty hard in the car outside her house and then they'd driven away together.

Every Shifter within viewing, hearing, and scenting distance would understand that Lindsay and Xav had gone to indulge in some mating heat. She'd been ready to be with Xav, had loved every second of what they'd done last night.

It had never occurred to her that she'd be putting him in danger.

Fucking wolves.

Lindsay strode toward the large two-story house Graham had commandeered for himself when he'd moved here. Eric hadn't opposed his choice, because he'd preferred to smooth the transition rather than fight Graham on every point. Eric was good at choosing his battles.

Lindsay just wanted to battle.

She marched onto the porch and banged on the front door. "Graham," she yelled. "Come out here."

The door was yanked open by a very small person who peered up at her with solemn gray eyes. "Hi, Lindsay. Are you okay?"

Lindsay rapidly dialed back her anger. "Hello, Matt. Is Graham at home?"

Many Shifters couldn't tell Matt from Kyle, his twin, but to Lindsay, the two cubs were very different. Lynxes were particularly good at scent, and the two little wolves, while remarkably similar, were each unique.

"He's here," Matt answered. "You're upset at him for endangering your mate, aren't you?"

Sheesh, did everyone in Shiftertown know about this? "He isn't my mate." Lindsay's eyes stung. "He might never be. Where is Graham?"

"I'm right here." Graham's rumbling voice came to them, followed by the bulk of the Lupine filling the entrance hall. "Matt, what did I tell you about throwing open the door before I'm downstairs?"

"I knew it was Lindsay," Matt said. "Lindsay's nice."

A yipping sound accompanied this statement as Kyle, in his wolf-cub form, gamboled down the stairs and joined his brother. Kyle danced around Lindsay's ankles, tail moving rapidly.

Even the adorable cubs couldn't dampen Lindsay's outrage for long. "Graham—"

"Did Eric send you?" Graham interrupted in his usual window-rattling voice. "Asshole was only supposed to tell you and your human to lie low."

Lindsay drew a breath, trying to make herself speak rationally. "First, I haven't seen Eric. Second, it's *your* Lupines who are trying to cause trouble." She folded her arms. "Third, Xav isn't my human. We're not together." She rapidly went over the past day and a half in her head and all the confusing emotions the hours had wrought. "I don't think."

"Bull crap. It's obvious you had sex with him last night." Graham scowled. "I'm trying to keep my Lupines calm, but they're furious with you, a fair-game female, for choosing a human. Especially *that* human."

To hell with being rational. "Why? Because Xav knows how to take care of himself? Because he's smarter than any

Lupine I know?" Lindsay glared at Graham to include him in this category.

"Because Xav's brother is mated to Eric's second," Graham all but shouted. "They don't want Eric gaining any more power. If Eric has family ties to every Feline Shifter in this town, the Lupines lose."

"That's the most ridiculous thing I've ever heard." Lindsay said in exasperation.

"We'd have been fine if they hadn't tried to shove two Shiftertowns together. It's a fucking mess, and I work every day to keep it untangled. You mating with one of Eric's Shifters is one thing. You mating with someone deeply connected with him is another."

"It's none of their business!" Lindsay pressed her palms to her chest. "*I* choose my mate, not your stupid Lupines. Even if Xav was connected to the head of Shifter Bureau himself, it's still my choice. I don't give a shit if some effed-up Lupines don't like it."

"Don't even joke about Shifter Bureau, especially not at my front door," Graham commanded. "Everyone on the street heard you."

"Like you're not yelling at the top of your lungs. Why should I care?"

"Listen to me." Graham quieted, and the authority that made him an undisputed leader cut through Lindsay's blustering. "I'm doing what I can, but these are pissed-off, half-wild Shifters whose chances at mating were cut in a big way when they were shoved into this Shiftertown. If you and Xav mate—officially, under sun and moon—they'll have to back off, whether they like it or not, and they know it. But the way things are now, they see Xav as an obstacle between them and you, one to be eliminated."

Graham took a step closer, and Lindsay's wildcat's heart pounded with instinctive fear. Graham continued, "Either you and Xav mate, Linds, and do it fast, or you give him up entirely and make sure everyone knows it. Any other choice, and they'll try to Challenge. Or maybe even not bother with the Challenge and go for the kill."

The cubs stared up at Graham, wide-eyed, and Lindsay swallowed. "Diego will never stand for that," she declared. "He's a dangerous enemy to make."

"No kidding. But half a dozen Lupines in mating frenzy won't think of anything but eradicating Xav until it's too late." Graham softened his tone until he sounded almost sympathetic. "You can't ignore this, Lindsay. You don't like it—and I don't blame you—but it's the situation. You say it's your choice? Then make one."

"You mean for the good of Shiftertown?" Lindsay tried to regain her resolve. "Well, for the good of Shiftertown, *you* should keep your wolves in line."

"She's right," a light voice came from inside. Lindsay peered past Graham and saw Misty, his mate, at the foot of the staircase, listening to every word. "The pressure shouldn't be on Lindsay."

"*I* know that." Graham's frustrated roar returned. "I'm doing the best I can. But this on-again, off-again thing with Xav is driving everyone wild. Is Lindsay fair game or not? Is Xav a threat or a friend? We're Shifters. Our emotions are pretty basic."

That was true. While humans might find compromises, Shifters would battle it out. Living in Shiftertowns had forced them to work things out more peacefully than they had in the past, but a beast hovered just below every Shifter's façade, danger waiting to explode.

There was danger inside Lindsay too, she hoped they all realized.

"I understand," she made herself say. "I'll give this some thought."

"What I mean is shit or get off the pot," Graham stated. "All right?"

"Nice metaphor, Graham." Lindsay looked him up and down. "I remember when *you* couldn't figure out what to do with your hots for Misty."

Graham flushed. "And I made the decision, didn't I? Call Xav. Work it out. Now, I have things to do."

Behind Graham, Misty rolled her eyes. She came down the stairs and out of the house before Graham could close the door, and caught Lindsay in a hug.

Misty was a small woman, and holding her was like embracing a fragile figurine, but Misty had a strength very few suspected.

"Don't let him get under your skin," Misty murmured into Lindsay's ear. "I think you know, deep down inside, what you need to do."

Lindsay found herself trembling. She returned the hug, wondering if the rest of the Shifters understood how wise Misty was.

"Thank you," Lindsay whispered.

Misty released her, and Lindsay wiped her eyes, wondering why she was suddenly crying.

Graham glowered from the doorway while Misty patted Lindsay's shoulders and gave her an encouraging smile. "Take care, sweetie."

"I will. See you, Graham." Lindsay turned her back, something she'd never, ever do to Eric, and walked away.

But Graham wasn't her leader, was he? Even so, it was difficult to make the defiant gesture—telling Graham plainly he wasn't the boss of her—to someone so seriously alpha.

One reason Lindsay had been attracted to Xav from the start was that while he was strong, and very alpha himself, he wasn't an asshole. Graham's wolves needed to learn that.

Lindsay paused at the end of Graham's front walk,

wondering whether to go home or out for a run. The cat inside her wanted to dash around until she was exhausted and then curl up and go to sleep. Things always looked brighter after a good nap.

Or, she could call Xav right now, explain the danger of him coming to Shiftertown ever again, and end it with him.

Not that she'd accept any mate-claims from annoying Lupines, but Graham was right. Until his frenzied Shifters knew whether Lindsay was mating with Xav or not, they wouldn't settle down to be their usual irritating selves. She was aware that Eric's unmated Shifters, though less demonstrative, wanted that answer as well.

The thought of telling Xav to stay away for good ripped a hole in her heart and flooded her eyes with more tears.

Lindsay started walking. She didn't know where she was going, and she didn't care. She strode down the street, heading for open country.

A breeze touched her ankles. Lindsay glanced down to see, through her blurred vision, two wolf cubs running in circles around her. They emitted baby howls when they felt her attention on them, tails wagging hard.

Matt and Kyle had come to protect her, she realized. To walk with her and keep her safe.

Lindsay became abruptly aware of watchers—from porches, from front windows, from shadows of thick mesquites that dotted the way. Hostile watchers, she sensed, likely the Lupines who'd threatened Xav or those who sympathized with them.

Some Shifters would welcome any excuse to start a war between Graham's Shifters and Eric's.

All because Lindsay didn't know what was going on in her relationship with Xav. So unfair.

She understood, though, that most Shifters would blame

her if Graham's Lupines caused trouble. Eric and Cassidy would not, but they'd have to deal with the mess.

"Shit!" Lindsay shouted to the air.

The cubs yipped in sympathy, their circles around her more enthusiastic.

She realized, after she'd gone another block, that the two were herding her back toward her own house.

"I'll be all right, guys, really," she tried to argue. "I'm more worried about *you*."

Kyle started to howl, a high-pitched, piercing noise. Matt's yipping increased.

Misty had once told Lindsay that the wolf cubs, in spite of their cuteness, were quite powerful Shifters, descended from hyper-strong Lupines of the past. They had abilities that Graham couldn't explain and probably more that nobody knew about yet.

But in Lindsay's eyes, they were still cubs. If one of the watching Lupines decided to attack her, he'd kick aside the little wolves without remorse.

"I'll go home," she assured them. "But only if you two go back to Graham and Misty. They need you."

The cubs utterly ignored her. Tails going like mad, they continued their enthusiastic circling, guiding her inexorably along her street and to her house. Lindsay sensed the watchers retreat, turning away to other things as though understanding they'd lost this round.

Matt and Kyle stuck to Lindsay until she reached her back door. When she leaned down to stroke their fur in thanks, they went wild, licking her face and yipping in joy.

They waited until Lindsay had gone all the way inside before they tore across the backyards, heading once more for Graham's house.

Lindsay watched them go with regret. The cubs were not

only protective, they were good at distracting her from despair.

She knew that once she'd retreated into the solitude of her own room, she'd have to face some hard truths, ones that might end in profound pain.

———

XAV AND NEAL SPENT THE MORNING TRACKING THE HELICOPTER, picking up its path from chance videos posted by campers and hikers, air traffic reports Neal hacked his way into, and a few calls to radio stations from those insisting they'd seen a UFO near Area 51.

Xav plotted the sightings, and they came up with a rough map of the helicopter's movements.

Brody supplied coffee and went on a donut run as Xav and Neal worked.

"You two about done?" Brody asked after they'd gone through half the box of donuts. "This is like watching paint dry."

"Not quite." Xav rolled back from the computer in resignation. Neal, who let nothing faze him, lounged in a kitchen chair munching on a chocolate-covered donut with multicolored sprinkles. "We have a direction the helicopter went, but not its final destination. We'll have to drive around looking for possible landing sites."

"Good," Brody rumbled. "Tracking, I can do. This computer stuff, not so much."

"You'll need Shifters," Neal said as he licked chocolate icing from his fingers. "More than the two of us, I mean, and more than Lindsay with her super-scenting abilities."

"Lindsay's out of this." Xav had decided that once Emma had given her report. "She'll argue, but I'm hoping we can find the guy and be done before she works up a head of steam."

Brody grinned. "I can think of ways you two can release some of that pressure."

Xav tried to stop his blushing, but by Brody's widening smile and Neal's quiet amusement, he failed.

"Lindsay's right," Xav observed dryly. "Shifters can't mind their own business."

"Hey, a mating is a celebration for us all." Brody sat his bulk on a chair that was *not* made for grizzlies and grabbed—what else?—a bear claw. "Congratulations."

"I don't know if it's heading anywhere beyond last night." Xav wondered why he felt so hollow admitting this. "Lindsay and I aren't exactly going steady."

"Going steady." Brody chuckled. "Do the kids still say that? I think she's settled on you, my friend."

Xav shook his head. "We're on-again, off-again. *On* never lasts long."

"Do you go out with other women when it's off?" Neal asked in curiosity.

Xav shrugged. "Sometimes. Nothing serious."

Neal spread his hands, one holding another donut, as if to say, *There you go.*

"I tried to break up with her the other day," Xav said. "For her own good, I told myself. But I couldn't stay away from her." He sighed. "I'm not sure if that's my fault or hers. Both, I guess."

Brody rolled his eyes as he finished off the bear claw and wiped glaze from his lips. "Humans. So fucked up. Just grab her and mate-claim her. She'll go from prickly to purring in no time."

"Shifters," Xav returned. "You think everything is so simple. What about Martin and Leah? Are they going to be thrilled if a human mate-claims their daughter? I get along fine with them, but that's because I'm only a friend with benefits right now. Nothing too momentous."

"What Eric will think is more important," Neal pointed out. "As leader, he has to make sure nothing rocks the Shifter-town boat."

"Even more complicated." Xav made a noise of exasperation. "I disagree that Eric's opinion is more important than Lindsay's family's, but as Brody has made clear, I'm not Shifter. All the Shifters respect Diego, but he's always been a commander. *I'm* the fun-loving little bro he has to keep out of trouble. I don't want to be in a situation where Diego has to fight my battles for me. He's saved my butt too many times in the past."

If Lindsay had been a human woman, Xav would have long ago suggested she move in with him, or he with her, if she preferred.

But then, if Lindsay wasn't exactly who she was, Xav might not have stuck around with her. He'd dated several women in the past who'd have been amenable to a long-term relationship, even marriage, and he hadn't pursued it.

After he'd met Lindsay, that had been it.

Last night, with her warm and sexy on top of him, had clinched the matter. There was no other woman for him but her.

Xav's cell phone pealed. When he saw the caller's name, he immediately grabbed the phone and left the room. The two Shifters craned to watch him all the way.

"Hey, Lindsay," Xav answered, unable to quench the delight in his voice. "What's up?"

"Hey, Xav." Lindsay's tone held sadness, and Xav's excitement diminished. "I'm going to say the four words you probably least want to hear. *We need to talk*."

CHAPTER TWELVE

When Lindsay emerged from the basement, where she'd taken her mother's suggestion and raced around the cage in lynx form awhile, her head was clearer, though her heart was heavy.

Xav hadn't arrived yet, but had promised he was on his way. Lindsay knew he'd have to head to Eric's to report on the helicopter's landing point, and she was fine with postponing the talk until after that.

She used the waiting time to visit Jinx, a Lupine woman who was actually nice—but then, she wasn't part of Graham's bunch. She and her mate lived in one of the larger houses, because they'd been blessed with nine cubs.

Four of the cubs had been Jinx's with a former mate, who'd been killed when Shifters had been rounded up. She'd met Joel, her current mate, in this Shiftertown, and they'd had five more.

Lindsay did want cubs at some point in her life, but she couldn't imagine wrangling *nine*.

On the other hand, Jinxie and Joel Soanes always appeared comfortable and content in their living room with its worn furniture, while their cubs, ranging in ages from two to twenty-five, roved around them. While twenty-five was adult age for a human, Clay, the oldest, was still considered a cub and would be until he had his Transition.

Joel and Jinxie were also perennially broke. Most Shifters had stashed away what wealth they could over the years, but the Soaneses ran through whatever they had trying to keep nine cubs fed and clothed. Cassidy and Eric helped them out monetarily from time to time, and Lindsay lent them moral support.

Today, however, visiting Jinx and family was more to bolster Lindsay's spirits than the reverse.

Lindsay didn't need to tell Jinx the source of her downer today, because Jinx already knew. The Lupine grapevine was swift—didn't matter that Jinx wasn't one of Graham's wolves.

"You and Xav will work it out," Jinx said in her calm tones as two wolf cubs wrestled over a soft toy between them. Jinx had warm gray eyes, tawny hair, and a kind smile. "Trust in the Goddess."

"How did you know it was right with Joel?" Lindsay asked. Joel wasn't there at present, off working to support his brood.

Lindsay tossed a ball at another wolf cub, who stalked it, pounced on it, and proceeded to chew it to bits.

"I didn't, not at first." Jinx took on a nostalgic expression. "Joel started helping out with my four, keeping them occupied so I could get things done. He came around more and more often, and finally, I said he might as well stay. He agreed, made the mate-claim, and we asked Eric to do the mate blessing."

Lindsay was certain there had been much more to it than that, but Jinx regarded her with the serene expression of a woman without many worries.

Trust in the Goddess. Presumably, She knew who should be together and guided them there.

Lindsay wasn't as certain. She only knew it was painful to have to sort through her feelings about the mate bond and her need for Xav.

A text from Xav telling her he'd just arrived at Eric's had Lindsay quickly rising. Jinx hugged her in understanding, then she and the cubs waved her off.

Lindsay returned home to grab the small backpack she'd prepared for the mission and took off across the yards. She sensed Xav's presence before she saw his telltale black SUV in front of Eric's house.

The connection she'd felt to him last night and this morning surged, and her inner cat purred with satisfaction. *My mate is back.*

Lindsay slowed her pace as she neared the house. The truth was, she didn't want to have this conversation with Xav, to explain that a Shifter and a human with connections to a Shifter leader was a volatile mix around here. To discuss with him about what they should to do.

Graham's advice to simply break it off would be cleaner and more final, Lindsay knew, but she couldn't bring herself to cut the ties without discussing it with Xav first. He should have some say in his fate.

Before Lindsay reached the Warden house, a large man walked out its back door and blocked her way.

Lindsay halted in surprise. "Tiger."

Tiger gazed at her from his tall bulk, his golden eyes holding mysteries. Tiger was larger than almost all the Shifters, only the bears matching him. His hair was striped black and orange, and his calm face belied the ferocious creature he could become.

Eric and Iona had rescued Tiger from tragic captivity a few years ago and brought him home. All of Shiftertown had been terrified of him, Lindsay included. The Morrissey family from the Austin, Texas, Shiftertown had taken him to their home, giving him a refuge. In Austin, he'd met the human woman, Carly, who was now his mate.

Lindsay had since learned that Tiger had a gentle heart. The way he protected and loved Carly and his cubs was a beautiful thing.

On the other hand, Tiger remained unpredictable and could be a formidable enemy when he chose.

"Lindsay," Tiger said after a quiet moment. "It will be all right."

Lindsay blinked. "What will?"

"You and Xavier. He is the mate of your heart, so everything will be all right."

Lindsay dissolved into nervous laughter. "You know what, Tiger? You're uncanny. You sense these things, do you?"

"Yes." Tiger gave her a nod. "Also, Xavier told me you wanted to talk to him."

Lindsay's heart thumped. "I'm so glad he's keeping our private life to himself. Why are you here, anyway? Is everything okay in your Shiftertown?" Her worry returned. "With Carly?"

"Carly is here with me, and she is well." The devotion in Tiger's tone pulled at Lindsay's heart. "Xavier said he needed help tracking someone, and I am the best tracker there is. We are discussing what I will do."

Tiger's assertion was not a boast. As Lindsay had mused not long ago, his help would be invaluable.

"In that case, I can go back home," Lindsay teased. "You all organize the mission and send for me when you're ready to go. Tell Carly I said hi. Better still, send her over. We can talk about you guys while you're working."

Tiger shook his head. "You are needed, Lindsay." He turned, gesturing with his big hand to the house.

Lindsay swallowed her trepidation and headed after him.

Carly was indeed in the living room, her musical voice

rising in conversation with Cassidy and Iona, who both crooned over Seth, Tiger's small cub. They all greeted Lindsay, but Tiger indicated Lindsay should follow him into the kitchen.

There, Diego and Eric hovered behind Xav where he sat before his laptop at the kitchen table. Eric and Diego turned to pin Lindsay with keen stares when she and Tiger entered the room.

Tiger stepped to the side, as though he could blend into the woodwork, and nursed a cup of coffee that had waited on a counter for him.

"Ah, Linds." Xav greeted her in his warm but offhand tones, as though there was nothing awkward between them. He turned back to the laptop, which held maps with colorful dots on them. "We've pinpointed a broad location where the helicopter might have landed. North of Death Valley Junction near the border between California and Nevada. Lots of wilderness to hide in there, so we decided it was time to call Tiger."

"I wasn't busy," Tiger said calmly.

"From there, our quarry might have been picked up and taken anywhere," Xav continued. "Or tried to hike out on foot, which is a bad idea, even in the middle of winter."

True, February temperatures could rise to the nineties during the day in Death Valley, though it was still bitterly cold at night. Plus, Xav was right—the area was vast. The helicopter had landed a long way from anywhere.

"Where do we start?" Lindsay asked. "At the landing site?"

Xav swiveled to face her. "*You* don't start anywhere. Tiger's agreed to help, so you can stay home and not wear out your paws."

Lindsay gazed right back at him. "We've had this argument before. AC hired *me*. I'm going, even if I don't like the idea of racing around Death Valley in the middle of the broiling afternoon."

"We will need her," Tiger rumbled from his corner.

"It's dangerous," Xav said firmly.

"We need her nose," Tiger continued. "Lynx Shifters have a superior sense of smell."

Lindsay pointed at Tiger. "What he said."

"Linds …"

"Forget it, Xav, I'm coming with you. AC is paying *me*, and I want the money."

Xav's eyes narrowed in both suspicion and surprise. "What for?"

Lindsay shrugged, evasive. "To buy new shoes."

"You have a lot of shoes," Xav said with a touch of amusement. "I mean, a lot."

"And your point is …?"

Xav rose from his seat, Diego and Eric wordlessly melting out of his way as he headed for Lindsay. Xav gripped her by the elbow and steered her from the kitchen and out the back door of the house. Thankfully, no one followed them.

Xav walked Lindsay briskly from Eric's yard and down the shared land behind the houses, saying nothing. Lindsay realized he was heading for the open desert beyond, where they'd gone before to have a discussion. That one had ended in disaster, and this one might be even worse.

Lindsay glanced around uneasily as they went, worried that Graham's Lupines might try to confront Xav while he was apart from Diego and Eric, but she sensed no one. Hopefully Graham was keeping his unruly wolves at bay.

Once they reached the fringes of Shiftertown, Xav released Lindsay and faced her. "You said you wanted to talk," he stated. "Never a good thing, as you implied. So—talk."

Lindsay's mouth went dry. She remained silent for a time,

while a cold wind blew her hair into her face, and Xav watched her with his intense, dark eyes.

She drew a breath, summoning courage. "We have to decide now." Her voice was faint, cracked. "Are we breaking up? Yes, or no?"

Xav's brows rose a fraction. "I tried to before, remember? It didn't exactly work."

"You didn't try very hard."

"I admit that. Neither did you." Xav's faint smile shot heat through her, as she recalled him over her in the dark, whispering *Damn, Linds. You're beautiful.*

"We can't keep on like this," Lindsay said, her chest constricting.

"I agree. Do you want to break up?"

"No." The word emerged with vehemence. Lindsay tried to compose herself. "But it might be for the best."

Xav's mouth tightened. "Why? I thought so before, but I've changed my mind, if you couldn't tell. You seemed fine when you left my house this morning. Why do you want to call it quits all of a sudden?"

"So Graham will cease giving me hell," Lindsay blurted before she could stop herself.

Xav's controlled expression became a scowl. "Graham? What the hell has he got to do with it?"

"Too many Lupines need mates." Lindsay tried to sound reasonable, but her voice shook. "Graham can barely keep them under control."

Xav regarded her in amazement. "Meaning if we break up, you're free to go to one of them? Is that what you want?"

Lindsay's eyes widened. "What? Hell, no. I'm not hooking up with a smelly wolf so Graham can keep the peace." She drew another breath to calm her agitation. "But Shiftertown is like a dormant volcano. Looks fine on the surface, but there's all this magma waiting to burst out. I'm giving the magma excuse to erupt, and I need to stop it." She waved her hands in frustration. "I'm not explaining well. You'd understand if you were Shifter."

Xav nodded, as though he understood well enough. He was also growing angry, his placid surface rippling like the aforementioned volcano.

"What you're saying is, you want to break up with me to keep things calm in Shiftertown."

"Yes." Lindsay swallowed, her throat aching.

"Who knew I was that big of a threat?" Xav asked in feigned astonishment. "Xav Escobar brings down Shiftertown because he likes going out with Lindsay Cummings. So much *power*."

Lindsay balled her hands. "This isn't a joke. Graham said *I* needed to make the choice, but he's wrong. We both do." She took a step back. "I'm really bad at this, Xav. Help me out here."

Xav sent her a quizzical glance. "You've never broken up with anyone before?"

"I never had the chance. I keep it casual." She hugged herself as the wind sharpened. "Best that way."

"Is it?" Xav closed the small distance between them. "Casual seems to be dissolving the glue that holds Shiftertown together."

"Casual means not making tough decisions," Lindsay said. "It means having fun, not heartache."

Xav moved even closer, his warmth masking the chill. "What did you say was our choice? Break up, or ... what? Keeping it casual is obviously out."

Lindsay swayed toward him, unable to resist the pull to his heat. "We either mate for life, or stop seeing each other. I know which one you'd prefer."

"Do you?"

Xav's voice went hard. He caught her hands that hung by

her sides and wound them behind her, trapping her against him.

Lindsay knew she could easily twist away, but she didn't want to. She wanted nothing more than to stand still while Xav's breath brushed her lips.

This kiss, when it came, was fierce. Lindsay rocked with the unexpected force, then she met Xav's kiss with a fervent one of her own.

His mouth was commanding, dominating, and Lindsay didn't care. This was Xav, and Lindsay wanted him with the whole of her heart and the whole of her body.

Xav broke the kiss just as abruptly and released her. Lindsay staggered, barely righting herself as her booted foot slipped on gravel.

Xav regarded her steadily, his chest rising with a sharp breath.

Then, without warning, he seized her by the hand and started striding back toward Shiftertown, pulling her in his wake.

"Xav. Wait a sec." Lindsay's protest was ignored. "Where are we going?"

Xav didn't answer. He towed Lindsay along the row of houses, while Shifters who happened to be outdoors watched with great interest.

Matt and Kyle ceased chasing each other behind Graham's house and came alert, ears pricked. They ran after Lindsay and closed in behind her.

Xav didn't stop until they reached Eric's place. Xav pulled Lindsay in through the back door and made for the living room, where Eric was expounding to Diego and Tiger. The ladies and cubs were still in the dining room, their lively conversation ceasing as Xav stormed in.

Tiger's head came up, his gaze snapping straight to Xav, not to Lindsay.

"Eric," Xav said in a commanding tone.

Eric, who now lounged in his usual place on the sofa, glanced up at him. Anyone not Shifter would think him merely curious about why Xav had burst in and interrupted him, but Lindsay saw the dangerous glint behind the quietness, the leopard ready to strike.

"What is it?" Eric managed to say patiently.

Xav turned to face Lindsay. He hadn't let go of her hand, and now he gripped both of them more firmly.

"I need you to hear something," Xav told Eric. "Lindsay Cummings," he stated to her with strength. "Under the light of the sun and before witnesses, *I claim you as mate.*"

CHAPTER THIRTEEN

L indsay's reaction was pretty much what Xav figured it would be. She stared at him in shock, her beautiful green eyes filled with incredulity.

What she'd do next, Xav wasn't certain. Swing around and walk off in scorn? Whack him upside the head and ask him what the hell he thought he was doing?

It was Lindsay's choice to accept the claim or tell him to leave her be and never come back. Which was what she wanted, right?

Xav knew what *he* wanted. Lindsay obviously assumed he'd dump her as soon as things grew complicated, but she assumed wrong.

After a few seconds of silence, while Xav and Lindsay fixed on each other, everyone else in the house—except Eric, Neal, and Tiger—erupted into noise.

Brody let out a "Woo!" that rattled the windows. Iona shrieked and leapt upward with cat grace, punching the air. Cassidy sped straight to Lindsay, lifted her off her feet, and spun her around.

"Oh, Lindsay, I'm so happy for you." The two ladies shared a tight embrace, Lindsay still bewildered.

Carly cheered with Iona, both of them joining Cassidy in a collective hug that swayed back and forth.

Eric had left the couch at some point—Xav never saw when—and now laid his strong hand on Xav's shoulder.

"Well done," he said quietly. "Welcome to the family."

Xav was technically already in the family via Diego, but Eric's grip conveyed a multitude of meanings. He was Lindsay's leader. If Xav did one thing to hurt Lindsay, he'd have to answer to Eric, even more than to Lindsay's parents, as Neal had posited. Eric took his job as protector seriously.

Big cats might look peaceful when lazing in the sunshine, but they were deadly, deadly creatures. *Never forget that,* Eric's solid grasp told Xav.

Diego moved to Xav's other side, as protective of his brother as Eric was of his Shifters. Diego was smiling, however, happy.

Tiger, who also wasn't one for shouting or dancing around, gave Xav a quiet nod. The big man turned and left the celebration, his glance at his own mate as he went the most loving thing Xav had ever seen.

Only Neal had remained calmly in the dining room on a chair he straddled backward. "You might give her a chance to answer," he observed.

The ladies unwound from Lindsay, all grinning, and tried to calm themselves, without much success.

"He's right," Cassidy said breathlessly. "But you two have been heating things up, and you scent-marked him, Linds. What are we supposed to think?"

Scent-marked? What the hell?

Diego looked as startled by Cassidy's announcement as Xav was, but Eric seemed pleased by this and relaxed his grip.

Lindsay gazed imploringly at her well-meaning friends.

"Give me a minute." She turned to Xav, beautiful eyes wide. "All right? Let me clear my head and think."

"Okay." Xav shrugged, pretending it didn't kick his ego that she didn't instantly burst into grateful tears and say *yes*. "This is important shit. Don't get caught up in the excitement."

Xav shouldn't either, he reminded himself, though didn't regret his spontaneous mate- claim one bit.

Not that spontaneous, actually. Xav realized he'd been contemplating this move for a while, even if he hadn't admitted it to himself.

Diego remained at Xav's side after Eric finally moved off. Diego didn't try to advise Xav or make any observations —he simply quieted the rest of the room with his patient gaze.

"We have a mission to run," Diego reminded them. "A hostage to find. Plenty of time for Lindsay to think while we carry on with it. Can you two work together without imploding?"

Lindsay straightened her back and wiped her eyes. "Of course. There's a job to do."

Xav wasn't so sure he wouldn't try to throw Lindsay over his shoulder and run off with her, but he nodded. "Sure. We can compartmentalize."

Diego's answering look held skepticism, but he didn't push it. "All right then. If Brody will quit doing a conga line by himself, we can continue."

Brody pirouetted in place, which was weird to see in such a big guy, then he clapped his massive hands together. "Sweet. Let's do this."

Lindsay said nothing. The glance she shared with Xav didn't reveal her decision, but it seared Xav to the core. This was, as he'd said, important shit.

No turning back now.

———

ERIC RESUMED THE BRIEFING, BUT THE MOOD IN THE ROOM WAS electric, the Shifters and Carly barely containing their excitement. The ladies and cubs surrounded Lindsay, carrying her in their bubble to the kitchen where much laughter ensued, probably at Xav's expense.

Tiger didn't return. As Xav knew what Diego and Eric were going to discuss, and Lindsay's friends had taken her over, he slipped out the back door and sought Tiger.

The large man stood in the middle of the common area, staring at nothing. Tiger often did this, so Xav didn't find it alarming.

Xav joined him, gazing around what had once been plain houses on barren lots that the Shifters had transformed into cozy homes. While Xav liked the house he'd purchased, with its luxurious fittings in the kitchen and bathrooms, it was very empty. There was a reason he found excuses to visit Diego in Shiftertown every evening, even beyond a chance to be with Lindsay.

"When I was a kid, I lived in a close community like this one," Xav said, whether Tiger was listening or not. "None of us had any money, but we all had friends. Everyone's mom looked after everyone else's kids, though we didn't realize it back then. I landed myself in lots of trouble, but I knew, beneath it all, that my friends and family had my back."

Tiger didn't answer. Xav figured he was lost in his own thoughts, until Tiger surprised him by turning his head and looking straight at Xav.

"This is the first place I saw after Iona rescued me," he said. "I'd never seen so many Shifters together, and none of them in cages. Eric let me stay in his basement, because I had a hard time getting used to being outside. I hadn't realized the world was so big."

"Yeah." Tiger's early existence had been bleaker than anyone could imagine. "I remember when they brought you in."

"They were afraid of me, the other Shifters," Tiger rumbled.

"I remember that too." Xav sent him a rueful grin. "So was I. You have to realize, no one had ever seen anything like you."

"I know." Tiger shrugged, unoffended. "I thought there would be nothing for me here except existence. When they sent me to the Austin Shiftertown, I thought the same. And then I met Carly."

Tiger's golden eyes softened, the brutal, very dangerous Shifter becoming the mate and father again.

"You knew right away, didn't you?" Xav asked him. He'd heard the story of how Tiger had found Carly broken down on the side of the road, and how she'd ended up assisting *him*, in all ways.

"I did." Tiger gave Xav a nod. "Carly argued with me about it, and the other Shifters said that wasn't how mating worked. It wasn't mate-bond-at-first-sight, they told me. But it was."

"You're a special Shifter, though." Xav glanced at the house where he could see Lindsay in animated conversation with the other ladies in the kitchen. Hands waved, bodies quivered in laughter. "I'm not a Shifter at all."

"But you know Lindsay is the one."

"I think she is, yeah. I do care for her. A lot."

Tiger regarded him steadily. "Humans never want to say exactly what they are feeling. Even Carly."

Xav huffed a laugh. "Because we'd all kill each other if we did. Look at what kind of shit goes on in social media. Not to mention face-to-face fights when people get drunk and lose their inhibitions. I was a cop for a while and saw it every day.

The best thing humans can do, most of the time, is shut the fuck up."

Tiger listened without changing expression. "You are speaking about anger and fear. I mean the deepest emotion of all, the tightest bond. It embarrasses you, so you pretend it doesn't matter." His eyes turned dark golden. "It does matter, and it should be talked about more than anything else. Shifters know this."

"Lindsay is Shifter, and she never mentioned the mate bond, or anything else regarding mating, until Graham more or less forced her to." Xav folded his arms, trying not to let her confusion at his mate-claim hurt him. "She didn't exactly leap to accept my offer in there."

"She did not expect it," Tiger said. "Lindsay is more guarded than most Shifters, because she grew up mostly alone. Not as alone as I did, but it takes a while to understand how to have a conversation."

"You're doing pretty well," Xav observed. "When you first came here, you had a hard time forming sentences."

Tiger nodded, again without offense. "I never had to speak much before. Iona and Cassidy helped me. Then Liam and Kim and their family did. Carly has helped me most of all. When I realized that she'd been there waiting for me, all the time I was in the cage, it made the darkness go away."

Xav blinked as moisture crept into his eyes. "I'm glad she was, big guy."

"She didn't know it. Neither did I. Shifters would say the Goddess knew, but I think it's even beyond that. We were made to be together." He focused his acute gaze on Xav once more. "So are you and Lindsay."

"I'm not sure she wants that," Xav said with regret. "She's being forced into this choice, but I think she'd prefer it if I vanished, so she can go back to her carefree life."

Tiger shook his head. "She does not understand or believe, but you are mates. You must make her believe it."

Xav grimaced. "Sure, like I can convince Lindsay do anything she doesn't want to. Growing up an only cub has made her more independent than anyone I know."

"*I* am independent. I need no one, can survive in impossible places all alone. That does not mean I want to."

"You have ties now," Xav pointed out. "You have Carly, Seth—who gets cuter every time I see him—and your daughter. Now your son-in-law and a grand-cub on the way."

"Yes." Pride surged in Tiger's eyes. "But I could survive physically if they were not here, as can you without Lindsay. You are very strong, for a human. That does not mean you should, or that Lindsay should survive without *you*. Carly likes to say we are two halves of a whole, better together than we are separately."

"Good way to put it." Xav felt a twinge of envy. He'd sensed that connection between Diego and Cassidy, Leah and Martin, and the other Shifters and their mates. He understood why Shifters sought the mate bond, but Lindsay had never seemed to.

"You and Lindsay are two halves," Tiger stated. "Make them whole."

Xav raised his brows. "Is that an order?"

Tiger considered, then gave him a nod. "It is a good order, so yes."

"The thing is, I agree with you." Xav heaved a sigh. "But how do I convince Lindsay?"

"She already knows. You need to persuade her acknowledge it."

"I think that's what I just said," Xav growled in exasperation. "Any tips on how? From an expert?"

Tiger regarded Xav for a long moment before he shook

his head. "You need to figure it out for yourselves. Now, I must return to my mate."

Without another word, Tiger turned around and marched toward the house.

Xav imagined gossamer tethers that surrounded him and Carly, pulling them together whenever they were too far apart.

"Some pep talk," Xav muttered to himself. "I have exactly the same information as when I started out."

"No, you don't." Tiger's voice floated back to him. Xav forgot the big man had amazing hearing.

And also, Tiger was correct. Maybe Xav did have more information. If Lindsay really wanted to be with Xav but for some reason feared to let herself, he could work with that.

Xav knew one thing for certain—he hadn't made the mate-claim lightly. He'd meant it. He wanted Lindsay in his life, for real and forever.

If she truly didn't want to accept, no matter what Tiger said, then Xav would make a clean break and walk away for good, which would mean avoiding Shiftertown as much as possible.

He'd never be able to be around the other half of his whole without feeling the wound of being torn from it.

Graham and his Lupines were right, Xav realized. Xav and Lindsay needed to fuse together or be completely apart. No in-between about it.

———

LINDSAY HAD NEVER BEEN MATE-CLAIMED BEFORE. SHE HADN'T been prepared for her wildcat's surge of triumph when Xav had said the words, the howl of glee that had wanted to escape her lips.

If she'd been in lynx form, she'd have dragged him off and made this mating official, in the most basic way.

As it was, with everyone standing in Eric's living room watching her, Lindsay's mouth had gone dry, and no words would come to her. Her conflicting emotions were all over the place, rendering her mute.

Fears had poured at her. First, she expected a bunch of Graham's Lupines to charge in and wait for her to accept so they could make the Challenge. She wasn't sure saying yes was the best thing for Xav's health right now.

Eric and Xav both were focused on this mission, so no mating ceremony would happen until it was over. Graham apparently was holding off his wolves for now, but Lindsay wanted to make sure the window between accepting and the mating ceremony would be small.

Also, Lindsay was still terrified the mating would not mean to Xav what it meant to her. She'd seen, in her previous Shiftertown, what had happened to a Shifter couple when one of the pair formed the mate bond and the other did not. It had been tragic and frightening.

The one who hadn't formed the mate bond spent a lot of time reassuring his mate that it didn't matter. Then he'd met a female Shifter he *did* form the mate bond with—both of them had—and he'd instantly gone off with her.

No one blamed him, including his mate, because mate bonds were sacrosanct, but the woman he'd left had folded in on herself. She'd gone back to her family, trying to carry on with her life, but she'd been broken. Lindsay had kept in touch with her clan when she'd moved to Las Vegas, and she'd learned the woman had found another mate, but no one mentioned whether that mate bond had ever formed.

Both had been Shifters in that case. There was no telling what would happen between a Shifter and a human, the humans in this room who'd formed the mate bond notwithstanding.

Even if the mate bond was not in question, Lindsay refusing Xav would keep him from Graham's bullying Lupines. If she rejected Xav, they'd have no reason to Challenge.

Either choice might break Lindsay's heart, but a rejection would at least keep Xav safe.

As Lindsay had dithered, speechless for once, Neal had noticed her hesitancy and reminded everyone that this was her choice, that she needed time to answer. He seemed to understand the problem more than the others, but then, he'd been gazing at Keira, the once-feral wolf Shifter, with bleakness in his eyes for a while now.

Not that Iona, Cassidy, or Carly had backed off. They'd pulled Lindsay into the kitchen for a celebratory beer and relived, in hilarious detail, how they'd reacted when *their* guys had mate-claimed them.

"Eric told me the mate-claim was necessary," Iona said, ice-blue eyes full of merriment. "For my own protection, of course. Nothing more. *Sure, sweetie.*"

"Everyone was so scared of Tiger," Carly recalled with a fond sigh. "They couldn't see how vulnerable he was. How gentle. Not that I raced to accept the mate-claim—I had no idea what the hell he was talking about." She laughed.

These ladies exuded happiness. They might have been startled or bewildered when they'd been mate-claimed, but they'd done what they'd needed to in order to be with the one they loved. Didn't matter if that one was Shifter or human, fierce leader or terrifying tiger.

Shifter rules and rituals had been incidental. The mate bond had not.

Lindsay shivered. The warmth in her heart had only

grown since she'd first noted it, spiking high when Xav had announced his mate-claim. *It* knew what she should do.

Once the rest of her could get her shit together, she'd know as well.

Diego popped into the kitchen. "Time to roll. Coming, Linds?"

"See, *Diego* lets me make my own choice," Lindsay said as she took up her backpack. "He doesn't go all command-y and protective-y."

"I am *not* getting in the middle of this." Diego moved to Cassidy, dropping a kiss to her mouth that promised passion when he returned.

Cassidy rested her head on Diego's shoulder. "Be careful, love," she whispered.

"Always." He slid his hand down to rest on Cassidy's abdomen. "Nothing will keep me from you, *querida*."

Lindsay realized she was staring at them, the Shifter in her drinking in their deep affection for each other. Carly and Iona had already retreated—Lindsay heard them in the living room having similar conversations with Tiger and Eric.

Lindsay closed her mouth, deliberately turned her back, and let her best friend have this moment alone with her mate.

Xav, Brody, and Neal were coordinating in the dining room. Lindsay marched up to them and inserted herself into the conversation.

"Where do you want me?" she demanded.

Xav's warm smile flashed fire through her, and Lindsay flushed as she realized her unintentional double-entendre. Xav didn't appear worried at all that Brody watched with high amusement, and Neal didn't disguise his Shifter nosiness.

"We'll talk about *that* when we get back," Xav said. "For now, stick with Tiger. You and he are doing recon, but the minute we find people who might shoot, you retreat. Got it? I'm not risking you."

Lindsay shrugged. "Sounds like a good plan."

Xav's smile vanished at her easy capitulation. He didn't trust Lindsay wouldn't do something impulsive, and he was right. If she needed to jump into the fray to keep Xav from being hurt, she would.

Lindsay gave into one of her impulses now. She stepped to Xav, never minding Brody and Neal, hooked her hand around the back of Xav's neck, and pulled him to her for a hot kiss.

When she eased away, Lindsay had the satisfaction of seeing Xav mystified. She gave him a little smile, shot a thumbs-up at the interested Brody and Neal, and sauntered away.

———

SHE WAS GOING TO DRIVE HIM INSANE, XAV THOUGHT. BUT A part of him decided he would enjoy it.

Lindsay insisted on riding in the SUV Xav drove, which was fine with him. Easier to keep an eye on her. She hopped into the back seat instead of the front, which was also fine. Xav would only be distracted by her curves and her sparkling smile if she sat next to him, and he'd need to concentrate on the drive.

Tiger and Brody rode in Diego's vehicle, but Neal joined Xav with two other DX guys chosen for the mission. They'd meet with more backup when they reached Death Valley Junction.

They timed the drive so that if they had to explore Death Valley itself, they'd enter it just as early evening cooled the land. Darkness wasn't an issue, because DX Security tech let them see all kinds of things at night, and Shifters didn't need light or gadgets to track their prey.

Lindsay didn't speak much during the drive, but then, neither did anyone else. Neal and the two men saved their energy for the hunt, and Lindsay peered out the window as though she had no interest in looking at Xav.

Xav's next conversation with her alone would be interesting. That is, if they gave themselves time to talk. He could think of much better things to do with his mouth.

He truly needed to settle this mate-claim, so every thought of her wouldn't be a distraction.

No, Xav would never be settled with Lindsay. Things would be as volatile in the future as they were now, no growing staid and comfortable once she accepted his claim.

Sounded good to him.

They crossed into California and reached Death Valley Junction in a little over an hour, meeting up with three other SUVs about a mile west of town.

One of the vehicles held AC, retrieved from the cabin. If they found Dean alive out here, he might be less terrified if he saw his brother among the geared-up men in black fatigues.

It also contained Emma, who'd bundled herself into a bulletproof vest and a warm hat against the now cold wind. Brody stared hard at her when she approached to be briefed.

"You look like a longshoreman who's expecting trouble," Brody rumbled.

Emma's eyes narrowed. "*You* look like a biker dude who'd rather be home watching TV."

Brody gazed down at his leather motorcycle vest and black T-shirt covering his hard stomach in surprise. "Of course I would. Bears like to be warm."

Emma turned away with the scorn only she could, and

Xav suppressed a laugh. Brody had no idea who he was tangling with.

They firmed up their plans, then the SUVs fell in behind Xav's as they rolled toward Death Valley.

Before they reached Furnace Creek, which held museums and accommodations for tourists, Xav turned onto a dirt road that wasn't on most maps. Neal, who had an electronic tablet in his hands, guided Xav to the area where they suspected the helicopter had landed.

The place they reached was remote, dry, and swiftly darkening. Land rippled in folds toward the distant, soaring mountains, and fell in the other direction to white salt flats of ancient lakebeds. With the sunset staining the sky a vibrant fuchsia, the vista was breathtakingly beautiful.

Also deadly for the unprepared. Xav's troops checked over their water, rations, gear, and clothing, from bulletproof vests to packed warm coats for the coming chill and boots solid against rocky soil. Everyone had an earpiece for communication, Lindsay tucking hers in without comment.

AC remained in a vehicle, his hands tied again, under the supervision of Emma and Neal. Neal had been correct about the man being docile. AC sat without fuss in the locked SUV, watching out of the dark window.

Twilight didn't linger. Soon, it was almost completely dark, stars emerging in the blue-black sky. Then even the hint of gold on the horizon vanished, and the temperature dropped. Xav zipped up his jacket and hiked toward the coordinates Neal had sent to his tablet.

His men fanned out, blending into shadows, becoming invisible against the terrain. Tiger, who didn't bother to blend, marched directly through the area Xav and Neal had pinpointed, Lindsay in his wake.

Diego joined Xav in a wide, dry riverbed near the lower slope of a steep, rocky escarpment. A second ridge rose on the other side of the flat area, a couple hundred feet away, a small canyon carved out by a long-gone river.

"Good pilot to be able to set down here," Diego observed, and Xav nodded.

After about twenty minutes of searching in an ever-widening circle, they at last found the telltale signs of a chopper—the unmistakable indentations of the landing skids and ripples of dust blown by the blades.

"Well, we were right that they were here," Xav said. "But where did they go? We found no trace of them beyond this," he finished in frustration.

Lindsay pivoted, a puff of dust rising from her boots. "We need to check over there." She pointed to a black shadow in the crevice of the closest ridge.

Tiger lifted his head and sniffed the air. "Yes."

Lindsay started off, and Xav jogged to catch up with her. "Carefully," he growled.

"It's all right." Lindsay didn't break her swift stride. "Someone's in trouble."

Before Xav could argue that she couldn't possibly know that, the unmistakable sound of a human voice drifted toward them. It was weak, cracked, and desperate.

"Help me."

CHAPTER FOURTEEN

L indsay scented the man's distress, overlaid with that of unwashed body, long before she heard the voice. He was dehydrated and weak, a fact natural predators would sense as well.

She moved unerringly toward the crevice in the ridge, moonlight brushing the variegated bands of color across the desert. Tiger caught up to Lindsay, passed her, and disappeared into deeper shadows.

Xav's voice sounded in Lindsay's earpiece. "Where'd you go, Tiger?"

Tiger didn't answer. Lindsay knew, more or less, where the frightened man was hidden, but Tiger, with his uncanny ability to track, had likely headed straight to him.

Lindsay crept forward, balancing easily on the uneven terrain, and peered into the crevice.

"I can see Tiger," she announced when she caught a glimpse of movement in the darkness.

She darted into the fissure, keeping a wary ear and nose out for any danger. Xav didn't try to prevent her, probably because Tiger, who could stop an enemy faster and more solidly than a tank, was ahead of her.

The narrow gap turned and twisted, walls growing closer as she went.

Lindsay caught up to Tiger in a spot where the rock walls nearly touched, except for a narrow gap near the ground. There was no way someone as large as Tiger could go forward from here. Lindsay slid around him and wriggled through the opening into a wider space on the other side.

A man huddled against the wall of the small cave beyond. His scruffy beard and hair were coated with dirt, his face and arms covered with scratches and blood. He raised his head when Lindsay squirmed into the niche, his eyes wide with terror and anguish.

"Found him," Lindsay announced into her communicator as she knelt beside him.

Tiger crouched down to peer inside then he unhooked an extra canteen he carried and passed it to Lindsay.

The man truly stank, which made Lindsay glad she wasn't in cat form, but his scent told her he wasn't Dean. She lifted the canteen to his lips, spilling a drop or two of water into his parched mouth.

The man's tongue worked, then he nodded that he was ready for more. Lindsay fed him slow sips until he could swallow a mouthful.

"Thank you," he whispered.

"What's your name?" Lindsay asked him.

"Jeff." He seemed to have to think about his surname. "Marshall."

"Can you walk out of here? If not, Tiger can carry you. He's super strong."

Tiger said nothing, only watched with his golden eyes. The man flinched in alarm then reassessed Lindsay.

"Y'all are Shifters," he announced.

"No kidding." Lindsay gave Jeff more of the water, as his weak hands couldn't hold the canteen. "How long have you been in here?"

"Don't know. We were flying around Wednesday night. I think. So, however long that's been."

Almost a week, without food, water, and blankets. Lindsay was impressed he'd survived as well as he had.

"Let's get you out of here." She put a hand under his shoulder and tried to help him to stand.

Jeff cried out and immediately collapsed. "Think I broke things."

Lindsay put her hands under his arms again, this time more gently, and half-carried, half-dragged him the short way to the opening.

She set him down again, and he grunted in pain. "You'll have to crawl through," Lindsay told him. "Sorry."

Jeff nodded once and rolled onto his belly. He had just enough stamina to inch himself forward, with Lindsay's assistance, until Tiger caught him and pulled him out.

Lindsay dove through once he was clear, somersaulting to rise to her feet. Jeff was staring up at the huge Tiger in sheer terror. He uttered a small scream when Tiger lifted him and cradled him across his shoulders.

Xav and the others were waiting when Lindsay and Tiger, with Jeff, emerged from the crevice. Xav immediately went to Lindsay's side, his eyes holding worry.

"Easy mission," she assured him. "Poor guy needs a hospital."

Tiger, without stopping, carried Jeff toward the waiting SUVs.

Xav slid his arm around Lindsay. "Nice work."

The warmth in Lindsay's heart became incandescent. She shrugged modestly. "Tiger pinpointed him."

"Don't sell yourself short. If Tiger hadn't needed your

help, he would have barreled in and out before any of us knew what he was doing."

Lindsay grinned. "You're right. I was awesome." She pumped one hand into the air.

Xav surprised her by pulling her close and kissing her on the mouth. A brief kiss, but one that fanned the fires.

"Don't get cocky," he rumbled, his breath hot on her cheek. "There might be more people out here to find."

"He didn't say anything about others," Lindsay said, not wanting to end this unexpected intimacy. "He might not have anything to do with Dean, or the helicopter."

"Don't bet on it. Did he look like a lost hiker to you?"

"Not really." Lindsay shook her head. "I wonder if the gang ditched him, and why."

"One way to find out."

Xav released her, the cold sharpening as he turned away. Lindsay swallowed her need and trotted after him.

Swift walking soon put them back at the SUVs. Tiger had Jeff sitting on the tailgate of one, wrapped in a thermal blanket, while a DX medic was alternately giving him oxygen and helping him drink more water.

Jeff stiffened when Xav approached then relaxed when he saw Lindsay with him. "Thanks," he told her.

"Sure." Lindsay shrugged. "What happened? Why were you in that cave by yourself? Where are your friends? And the helicopter?"

Both Xav and Diego shot her annoyed glances, which Lindsay ignored. They needed to know, didn't they? Lindsay's direct questions would save a lot of time.

"Copter crashed," Jeff surprised her by saying. He gestured weakly. "Out there. Somewhere."

"Shit," Lindsay said in shock. She hadn't smelled burning or fuel, so either the helicopter had gone down miles away or the remorseless wind and sun had stripped away the odors.

Neal approached, sword on his back, gripping a still-bound AC by the arm. Emma and Brody closed in on AC's other side. The group stopped several yards from the SUV but close enough so that AC could see the man sitting on the lowered tailgate.

AC betrayed no recognition of Jeff. Humans could keep their emotions from their faces, but slight movements and scent betrayed them to Shifters. However, Lindsay could tell AC had never met the man. Jeff's eyes widened a bit when he saw AC, which might mean *he* had seen AC before, even if AC didn't recall it.

"Everyone got out," Jeff said to Lindsay. "There were three of us and the pilot. I was trapped under debris. They helped me free but I couldn't keep up with them walking back to the road, so they left me behind."

"Seriously?" Lindsay demanded in outrage.

Jeff nodded. "They parked me outside that place you found me, told me to take shelter there, and they'd send help." He trailed off bitterly, slanting a glance at AC. "I guess they never did."

"Total bastards," Xav said, in a tone that didn't bode well for whoever they were.

"Well, the dude I work for is pure evil," Jeff said. "I should have known better than to sign on with him, but I needed the money."

"Give me his name," Xav said. "We'll find him and explain why he shouldn't have left you behind."

Jeff moved uneasily. "Who are you guys?" He looked over Xav and the other DX men, taking in their dark fatigues and tracking gear. "You aren't cops. You work with Shifters."

"We're your fairy godmothers," Xav told him. "You won't have to worry about retaliation."

"Are you mercenaries?" Jeff's curiosity grew. "Doesn't matter who you are, though. I'm not a snitch."

"What about Dean?" Lindsay asked him. "Was he in the helicopter? Did he go with the others?"

Jeff frowned, his puzzlement true. "Yeah, he did. He wasn't hurt." He directed his next words at AC. "What are you doing here? You working with these guys now?"

AC still had his hands bound, but as Neal stood half in front of him, Jeff likely couldn't see that.

"Sort of," AC said. "Where did your friends go?"

"*Not* my friends. And hell if I know where they are now. We were moving base. Too dangerous to stay in the old one after we stole all that cash. I don't even know where." Jeff broke off unhappily. "I'm not high up enough in the hierarchy."

"We can find them," Xav said without worry. "Tell me who I'm looking for, specifically. Would assist me if you can tell me what hideout you were moving *from*."

"Don't you know?" Jeff gestured at AC. "You have him. He can give you the information, and I'm off the hook. Come on, man," he said to AC. "Help me out."

Xav glanced at AC in suspicion, but AC remained blank-faced. Lindsay scented something wrong, but AC still betrayed no recognition of Jeff.

"Let's get him to a hospital," Xav told his medic. "Maybe he'll be more forthcoming when he feels better."

The medic nodded and started wrapping his stuff to put away. The minute he moved from Jeff, the man amazingly tried to run.

He made it a few hopping steps before he yelped in pain. Lindsay, Xav, and the medic leapt after him, then Lindsay heard a shout behind them.

AC had lunged forward, breaking from Neal and hurtling himself at Jeff. Neal snarled and ran for him but not before AC jabbed the taser he must have lifted into Jeff's shoulder.

Jeff gasped at the impact, shuddered, and collapsed.

Lindsay caught him and gently lowered him to the ground, the medic reaching to help.

Lindsay rose to find AC waving the taser menacingly, keeping Neal and Brody at bay. "He's one of the bastards who took my brother," AC snarled. "He doesn't deserve to walk out of here."

"He couldn't have anyway," Xav said dryly. "He has a broken leg."

AC's eyes held rage. "I'd have shot him if I'd had a real gun. I think I'll just hang on to this toy one. Tell your wolf boy to back off or he gets it next."

"Drop it," Xav advised. "Or one of us *will* shoot you—with a real gun, as you call it."

"No, you won't. You're not cops anymore, and I can have you arrested for assault. I can turn you in for just threatening me. Not to mention kidnapping and confining me against my will."

"Are you shitting me?" Xav demanded. "And here I was feeling sorry for you and your kid brother."

"Oh, we'll still hunt for Dean," AC said. "When this guy wakes up, we can beat his whereabouts out of him. Let me hang onto this so I can defend myself, and we'll be good."

Xav scowled. All eyes were on him, including Diego's, letting him make the decision about what to do with AC. Even Neal had halted, waiting for Xav's command.

That meant no one was paying attention to Lindsay, and no one noticed when she started her run. A few heartbeats later, she was whizzing past the startled AC, too fast for him to react.

Lindsay sprinted into the desert beyond the SUVs, then spun around and held up the taser in triumph, moonlight glinting from it. "Score!"

"Thank you, Linds." Xav grinned at AC, now in Neal's firm

grip once more. "This is why it's good to have an amazing girlfriend."

Girlfriend. Well. Not *mate* yet, but Lindsay decided to take the win.

She studied the taser as though fascinated by it, then she sauntered to Xav and handed it off to him. "You have that. I don't like weapons. Don't need them." She mimed raking her claws in the air, smiling at AC.

The man scowled but went quiet again. Plotting something, Lindsay decided. From her exchanged glance with Xav, he thought so too.

Xav's praise stirred her mating need. Lindsay did another claw rake in his direction then ambled away, but her pretense at being cool couldn't stop the yearning boiling away inside her.

————

XAV KEPT LINDSAY CLOSE AS THE TEAM SPLIT UP, ONE TO TAKE Jeff to the hospital and AC back to DX for more questioning, the other to search for the crash site to see what it could tell them.

Diego led the contingent to return to Las Vegas with the captives—Emma, Neal, and Brody going with him. Xav headed up the search for the helicopter, with Lindsay and Tiger to assist.

The man AC had stolen the taser from was put onto Xav's team, and he immediately tried to resign.

"I let you down," the blond man named Mitchell said. "He must have lifted it when we were pulling him out of the SUV. You'll have my letter in your inbox in the morning."

Xav shook his head firmly. "No, you won't. You'll help us track this crash site, and suck it up. You won't be given guard duty for a while, but we're not unforgiving. Learn from your mistakes and do better."

Lindsay listened to this, her head cocked, as though judging Xav's decision. Her scrutiny was unnerving, and her closeness didn't help.

Mitchell was chagrined that AC, a professional criminal, had distracted him, but Xav felt forgiving for two reasons: One, if no one had given Xav a second—or third, or fourth, or fifth—chance when he'd been younger, he'd no doubt be in prison even now. Two, Lindsay had been distracting the hell out of him all day. If Xav had been the one close to AC, *his* taser would likely have fallen into AC's hands, or possibly a more deadly weapon. AC was tricky, and Mitchell needed the wake-up call.

Lindsay's quickness has solved the problem, and Xav's pride in her surged. Sometimes her unpredictability was an asset.

Xav had to be honest with himself—he loved that about her, even while she worried the hell out of him.

He made himself focus as they spread out, half of Xav's men on foot, the others in the SUVs on roads that could hold them. They didn't have the vehicles to cross the desert floor, so if they found nothing tonight, they'd return in the morning with ATVs.

Before they went far, Tiger broke from Xav's search pattern and struck out across the uneven ground. The others halted in surprise, but Xav didn't bother to call Tiger back. When the big Shifter tracked, it was best to let him go.

Lindsay peered after Tiger, her nose twitching. "I think I know where he's heading." She beamed Xav a smile. "Time to shift."

She ducked with her backpack behind a rocky outcropping, and before long emerged in her lynx form. She brushed once around Xav's legs then took off after Tiger.

Xav admired how she bounded effortlessly through the darkness, no rocks, holes, or slippery dust slowing her down. Moonlight streaked her fur silver, the tufts on her ears almost glowing.

Xav and the other men scrambled less elegantly in her wake. Tiger hadn't shifted at all but simply strode into the desert, sure-footed in combat boots.

It wasn't clear just when Tiger disappeared. One moment he was moving along the rising ground, the next, he was gone.

Lindsay loped up a low hill and paused at the top, silhouetted by moonlight. Through the night-vision goggles Xav had snapped on, she glowed hotter than anything else around him.

Lindsay glanced back at Xav, as though urging him onward, then she too disappeared.

"Lindsay." Xav didn't know if she still had her earpiece, though she couldn't answer him through it even if she did.

Xav headed straight for where he'd seen her last, his men falling in behind him. He felt a pull to her, even when he couldn't see her, couldn't hear her, as though she'd tossed an invisible rope to him.

Come on, Xav. Keep up.

She hadn't really said that or projected it into his head— Xav didn't think. But he knew that's what she'd been conveying when she'd glanced back at him from the ridge.

He scrambled up the slope where she'd waited to find that it ended at the edge of a steep drop. Below him lay a smooth stretch of desert floor, another dry lake bed whose sands spread out in a pale smudge.

In the middle of this smudge lay a pile of debris. Lindsay and Tiger stood on either side of it, contemplating it in silence.

Xav pushed up his goggles and searched for a way down,

finding the cut of a dry wash that snaked to the bottom of the steep hill. Paw prints were impressed into the wash's dust, so he knew Lindsay had taken this route.

Xav smothered curses as he slipped and slid along in her wake, wishing he had the nimbleness of a Shifter. Grunts and smothered growls behind him told him his men weren't thrilled with the path either.

They made it to the bottom without mishap, and Xav led his men cautiously toward where Tiger and Lindsay waited.

The remains of a helicopter, an R44, Xav could see, lay on its side, parts from its twisted blades scattered on the ground around it. The pilot had tried to set down in the lake bed but hadn't been entirely successful.

The copter hadn't caught fire, though these models had that history, and obviously the men had all managed to escape. Jeff must have been in the seat that hit the ground inside, with the frame bending around it.

Thankfully Jeff's fellow passengers hadn't been callous enough to simply leave him there. Though if they'd realized then how injured he was, Xav thought darkly, they might have.

Dean had been with them, Jeff had said. Though R44s only sat three and a pilot, and Jeff had been hurt, Dean must not have been able to get away from the other two. He'd been forced to walk out with them to whoever had come to pick them up.

That the three men had been retrieved, Xav had no doubt. If not, Xav's team would have found their bodies littering the way to the crash site.

"Why did they come here in the first place?" Xav wondered. "If they were moving to a new compound, why fly out to the middle of nowhere? Were they setting up some-place near here?"

"That Jeff guy might know," Mitchell said, sounding more

like his usual self. "Though if he's low in the hierarchy, as he claims, they wouldn't necessarily tell him."

"AC tased him before he could say very much. I have to wonder why." Xav moved to Lindsay as he contemplated the sad remains of the copter. "Smell anything interesting?" he asked her.

Tiger was moving aside the remains of the door that had stuck into the air. He leaned over the body of the helicopter and peered inside.

"Careful," Mitchell told him. "There might still be fuel leaking. Sparks can trigger a fire."

Tiger ignored him. He'd know how to prevent the remains catching fire—the man knew how to do everything else, so why not this too?

Lindsay quietly left Xav's side and joined Tiger. She leapt softly onto the top of the wreck, it moving not at all with her weight, and delicately sniffed the interior.

When Tiger lifted himself away from the door, Lindsay slipped past him and dropped inside.

Xav watched in horror as the entire helicopter groaned with the impact of her landing and slowly rolled over on its rounded frame, trapping Lindsay inside.

CHAPTER FIFTEEN

L indsay! *Shit.*"
Xav sprinted to the helicopter, panic giving him a burst of speed, his men pounding behind him.

Tiger put one hand on the fuselage and easily pushed it upright. Lindsay slithered from the small opening he made, shook herself out, then looked around with mild surprise at the gathered men.

What?

Xav didn't imagine the word this time. He read it in her eyes.

"Damn it, Linds, what the hell were you thinking?"

Lindsay walked to him with the pace of a cat who didn't give a crap what the humans were yelling about, and dropped a small, rectangular package wrapped in brown paper in at his feet. Then she sat down and licked her paw, brushing it over the side of her face. One of her ears turned inside out as she worked.

Xav leaned down and picked up the package, tore a corner of it with his gloved finger, and peered inside.

A cluster of hundred-dollar bills met his gaze. He stared

at it in surprise but not disbelief. The kind of men AC described as having taken Dean were accustomed to toting large amounts of cash.

The package was fairly small, which could mean it had been left behind by mistake, missed as the passengers were trying to scramble the hell out of the helicopter.

There was probably five thousand dollars in here, Xav guessed. Had this been dropped, unnoticed, because they'd carried out a bunch more packages like it?

This was a good find, but still, Lindsay had taken a stupid risk. *We'll talk later,* he promised with a silent glare.

Lindsay seemed to understand, because she rolled her cat eyes and turned her back on him.

"Tiger," Xav called to him, holding up the packet. "Any more of this in there?"

Tiger calmly ripped the rest of the door off and wedged it under the copter to keep it stable. He leaned inside and did a quick but thorough search.

"No," he said when he emerged. "No personal effects either. No phones, no wallets, no dropped IDs. Nothing to identify anyone."

"Was he in there, Linds?" Xav asked her. If Jeff had been telling the truth, Lindsay would have scented Dean among the passengers.

Yes. Lindsay gave him the barest nod, focusing tightly on him.

Tiger watched the two with enigmatic eyes. "No one in the helicopter was a captive," he announced.

Xav regarded him in surprise as the rest of the men fell silent behind him. It would be useless to ask, *Are you sure?* because Tiger always was.

Lindsay had moved to Xav's side, her warmth cutting the chill of the night. The look on her face said she agreed with Tiger.

"Stockholm syndrome?" Mitchell suggested.

"Dean has become a willing prisoner?" Xav mused. "Decided to join them instead of fighting them? Or is he faking, gaining their trust so he can escape?" He heaved a sigh. "More things we'll have to grill Jeff about when he comes out of it. No wonder Jeff sounded surprised when we asked about Dean. Maybe to him, Dean was just one of the team."

No one had any further contribution to this statement. They couldn't know until they questioned Jeff or found Dean.

Tiger, finished with his report, had returned to studying the debris. February wind swept down from the ridge and made Xav shiver. Must be nice to have a fur coat, he thought, glancing at Lindsay. He swore she looked smug.

"All right, let's call it a night," Xav said. "I don't think we'll learn anything more out here. Take some photos, pinpoint the wreck's location, and we'll call it in to the local police. This, I'm going to study some more." He hefted the package then tucked it inside his coat.

"Or take your girlfriend to Cabo," another of the men joked.

"Sounds really nice, but no," Xav said regretfully. DX Security maintained a reputation for staying on the right side of the law. He'd investigate where the money came from and turn it over to the Las Vegas police to take it on up the chain.

Lindsay began padding toward the ridge she'd climbed down, already finished. Xav gave a few more commands, then they scrambled back up the hill, Tiger assisting those who slipped or struggled. They hiked back to the nearest road, where Xav had radioed for the drivers to meet them.

Lindsay had run ahead, and by the time they reached the rocks behind which she'd shifted before, she came walking out from them, fully clothed and human, carrying her backpack.

Xav called in the helicopter crash to the sheriff of that county—by his GPS, the crash site was just outside the national park, and so the problem belonged to either Inyo County, the State of California, or the local tribal police. The lucky person who answered the phone at the sheriff's department wanted a lot of details, and by the time Xav was finished —leaving his phone number and promising he'd be available for more questions—the SUVs were loaded and ready to go.

Lindsay rode with Xav and again said very little. Tiger was quiet, but this was normal. Lindsay was usually a chatterbox.

When they reached DX Security, Xav had to report to Diego and couldn't corner Lindsay for a talk. He asked Neal to make sure she got home safely, and then she was gone before Xav had time to say goodbye.

This was one reason why he'd avoided becoming serious with Lindsay, Xav reminded himself as he strode to meet Diego outside the interrogation room where he'd been holding AC. His job didn't exactly have regular hours. Xav couldn't leave Diego with all the work to go sort out his love life.

Tiger's unnerving stare told Xav he thought he should.

Xav tried to ignore him while he and Diego stepped into Diego's office, where Xav briefed him in more detail on what they'd found, including Tiger's assertion that Dean might not have been a captive at that point.

Diego digested all this then told Xav that AC had at least given them a possible location of the former hideout the gang was moving from. Diego had assigned men to check it out.

Jeff was in the hospital with DX men to watch over him in case his colleagues found him and decided to keep him from talking.

The two brothers returned to the interrogation room once they'd exchanged information, where AC was being guarded by Brody and Tiger.

AC could steal another taser and try it on Tiger all he wanted, Xav thought with faint amusement, but it wouldn't matter. Tiger would shrug off the shock and break the taser into tiny pieces. By the AC's uneasiness, he realized this.

When Tiger shut the door, Xav wrinkled his nose. Lindsay was right—it got ripe in there quickly.

AC still showed no remorse about attacking Jeff. "He's part of the gang who kidnapped my brother," AC growled when Diego began his questioning. "He didn't care."

"Did you recognize him?" Xav asked.

"No." AC shook his head. "Never seen him before."

Tiger had situated himself near the door so anyone trying to get out would have to pass him. He nodded to AC's assertion, indicating the man wasn't lying.

AC risking tasing Jeff meant he was up to *something*. He might be honest about not knowing the man, but he could be concealing the truth about many other things.

For now, it was late, and Xav was growing tired of dealing AC. "You get to stay our captive until we find Dean," Xav told him.

"Then it's off to be arrested for what you did to Xav," Diego put in, his tone brooking no argument.

AC shrugged. "Fine by me. Your house, your rules. But only when Dean is safe."

Xav watched him closely, but AC was too practiced to give away his secrets. He'd try to escape at some point, Xav decided. He wouldn't be AC Parkes if he didn't.

Xav left Diego organizing the transfer of AC back to the cabin—Brody and Tiger would settle him in, and Neal would reprieve Tiger later.

AC went quiet under Tiger's stare, meekly letting himself be carted out for the drive to Mount Charleston.

Xav shucked his vest and fatigues, locked away his weapons, and stashed the bundle of cash in the safe. By the time Diego returned to the building, Xav sat at his own desk in jeans and sweatshirt, reluctant to return to his empty house. He was equally reluctant to drive back to Shiftertown, where Lindsay's parents and other Shifters would be watching, wondering if they would soon have a mating celebration or not.

Diego paused in Xav's doorway. "Go find Lindsay," he said. "Obviously you have things to sort out."

Xav leaned back in his chair, lacing his hands behind his head. "I thought making the mate-claim would calm things down, but it's just stirring me up. I don't want to be anywhere Lindsay isn't, but she drives me insane when I *am* with her."

Diego grinned. "Welcome to life with a Shifter. I hate to say this, bro, but it will never calm down. She'll always keep you on your toes, and you won't want it any other way."

Diego and Cassidy were deliriously happy, Xav had to admit. "I wish she'd have answered me," Xav said. "I'm not sure whether to rejoice or worry."

"Worry." Diego nodded. "Always. But enjoy it."

"Thanks. I appreciate your support."

"And don't wait too long to tell Mamita. You know, so she doesn't kill you. You're still young. Have your whole life ahead of you."

"Love you too, *hermano*."

Diego's grin became a laugh. "Yeah, you do."

Emma chose that moment to appear, a draft from the closing front door announcing her entrance.

"You guys are so cute," she said. "Don't let me interrupt the moment."

Diego stepped away from Xav's office door but didn't lose his smile. "What have you got, Ems?"

"I already found out where the money came from." Emma stated this matter-of-factly, with no implied boasting about how quickly she'd found the connection. "Money-laundering operation out of California that tried to move into Vegas territory. Needless to say, they weren't successful. Another gang waylaid them, relieved them of all their cash, and ran them out of town. Took a couple million off them, rumor goes."

"This waylaying gang is the one that has Dean?" Xav asked.

"No one admitted to knowing the perpetrator, which I found interesting," Emma said. "Means my contacts aren't afraid of the California gang returning but *are* afraid of the ones who vanquished them. One of my old friends told me— in person, not on the phone, only way he'd speak to me—that it was indeed Jeff's gang. He says its leader is seriously ruthless. If Dean is in his clutches, I suspect he's not getting away easily."

"Does your friend know whether Dean's joined them?" Diego asked.

Emma looked surprised at the question but shook her head. "He doesn't know much more, except that they've deserted their old headquarters. In his opinion, they'll use all the money to buy a mansion and live the good life."

"Or they're stashing the cash until the attention dies down," Xav suggested. "Somewhere they have to reach by helicopter? I thought maybe they were flying Dean out to kill him, but in that case, they'd have left his body at the crash site to make it look like he died in the accident. But if they didn't intend to kill him, why take him along?"

"Either he really has joined them, or they need him for some reason," Diego said.

"To get to AC?" Emma wondered.

"Possibly," Diego said. "Maybe that's why AC isn't trying harder to get away from us, and why he shut Jeff up. Could be he suspects they're dangling Dean as bait, and he wants to spring their trap, with DX Security as his backup," he finished wryly. "Thanks, Emma. I appreciate the extra effort. Now, both of you, get out of here. I'm going home. We all have lives."

Emma didn't hesitate. "Yep. Night is young. Want to go have some fun, Xav? Call Lindsay, and we'll party."

"Maybe I should head up to the cabin," Xav said without moving. "If Emma's hunch is right that the gang is using Dean to lead them to AC, we should make sure he's safe."

Diego raised his brows. "If you think anyone is getting past *Tiger*, you're losing it. You being there or not isn't going to make a difference."

He had a point, Xav conceded. Xav also had to admit he was looking for excuses to avoid confronting his suddenly complicated relationship.

"Go talk to Lindsay," Emma said. "Don't be a chickenshit. Yes, I know about the mate-claim. Brody told me."

"So nice to have privacy." Xav heaved himself up, telling himself that Emma was right. "Okay, okay. I'll go. Where? My business."

He grabbed his jacket and headed out of his office. Xav was usually the last to leave the building, the one who locked up, but he sensed Diego wouldn't let him do that tonight.

Diego and Emma stood back to let him stride past them out the door, and Xav pretended to ignore their knowing grins. He made for the back parking lot, shrugging on his jacket against the chill when he made it outside.

Lindsay emerged from the shadows and fell into step next to him.

"Shit." Xav jumped, the jacket settling on his shoulders. "I thought you left with Neal."

"I told Neal I wanted to wait for you." Lindsay slid her hand up Xav's arm as though she couldn't stop herself. She wore only the light sweatshirt and cargo pants she'd dressed in for the mission, no coat in sight, but her touch was warm. "He understood. Mating frenzy is a real thing."

Xav's heart beat faster. "Is it?"

"Sometimes happens after a mate-claim." Lindsay's hand moved to his shoulder, turning him to her. "The Goddess speeds up our instincts. Or something. I don't know. I only know it makes me want to do this."

She dragged him to her for a sudden and satisfying kiss, one that cut the chill of the breeze. By the time Xav caught his breath, she'd twined herself around him, her body hot.

"How about we take this inside?" Xav whispered as he leaned to nibble her enticing earlobe.

"Emma and Diego are still in there."

Xav laughed softly, his choice of where to go this evening suddenly settled. "I meant to my house. Away from prying Shifter eyes."

Lindsay hesitated, but Xav sensed it wasn't because she didn't want to continue what they'd started. He had the feeling she was ready to pull him into the bushes that lined the iron fence around their property and get on with it.

Xav's heartbeat sped even more imagining them sweaty and laughing as they tried to have sex with branches scratching at them.

"Fifteen-minute drive," he promised.

"Mm." Lindsay kissed him again, licking across his lower lip. "I might be able to hold it in that long."

"I'm willing to find out." Xav took her hand, and they started for his car at a run.

CHAPTER SIXTEEN

L indsay decided that curbing herself for the drive was too difficult. By the time Xav pulled into his driveway, she had his pants open and her hands playing with the warmth inside.

Xav drove into the large garage and shut down the engine. Lindsay barely noted that they'd stopped. His cock was stiff under her touch, sending her need soaring.

Before Xav could say a word, Lindsay lowered her head to his lap and took him in her mouth.

The groan Xav emitted made her wildcat purr. Lindsay traced him with her tongue, tasting the hot glory of him. She suckled, which made his groans louder and more desperate.

Xav's hips moved, his hands in her hair. "Linds. *Shit.*"

Lindsay continued relentlessly. Xav went back against the seat, his hips rocking. He furrowed her hair with strong fingers, as though he resisted pushing her farther onto him. Lindsay obliged his silent wish by taking him all the way.

The light that had come on in the garage when Xav opened the door clicked off, sensing no motion outside the vehicle. Lindsay was glad of the darkness—she had no need of light to see Xav wanting her.

Xav placed a firm hand on Lindsay's shoulder and drew her off of him. He was still hard, nowhere near sated, and Lindsay smiled at him.

"I said, let's take this *inside*," Xav said. "My garage doesn't count."

"Outside is good, though," Lindsay said breathlessly. "Maybe we could go up to the cabin once AC is gone, and play in the woods."

"In February in the freezing snow." Xav grinned. "Actually, that does sound kind of fun. But for now ..."

Xav fastened his jeans and hit the button to close the garage door. Not until it was fully closed did Xav climb out. He came around to open the passenger door for Lindsay before she could jump out on her own, then he slid his arm around her and led her into the house.

Once in the back hall, the door locked behind them, Xav backed Lindsay into the wall. His kiss held all the built-up tension she'd put into him with her play, and she smiled into the kiss.

He'd take her right there, she thought, her body rocketing with excitement. Any moment, he'd undo her clothes and his, thrusting into her and relieving the ache that had been building all night.

To her disappointment, Xav broke the kiss and backed away, drawing a long breath. "I need a shower," he said. "I'm coated in desert."

Lindsay brushed at dust that lightened his hair. "It's sexy."

Xav laughed. "To you, maybe." He turned away and strode through the kitchen to the hall on the other side, where he looked back. "Coming?"

Lindsay zipped to him faster than when she'd rushed AC

to grab the taser. Xav continued his laughter as he caught her hand and towed her into the bathroom.

He let the shower warm as they undressed each other, Lindsay's clothes falling away as fast as she tore off Xav's. She'd have to buy him a bunch more shirts if she kept shredding them like this.

Xav's large bathroom had a walk-in shower, the kind with no annoying doors or shower curtains to get in the way. He had a deep tub as well, which Lindsay thought would provide another place for fun.

For now, she let him guide her into the shower, the water quickly wetting their skin. Xav was right that dust had gotten inside his shirt to coat his chest and arms with dust, which Lindsay soon washed off with a good lathering of soap.

Xav applied soap to his hands and then skimmed them over Lindsay's body, sliding easily across her breasts and back, down to her buttocks and between her legs.

Lindsay growled with satisfaction as Xav lifted her leg over his arm, opening her for his fingers. Sensations chased through her, beautiful need making her hot, then shiver, then hot again.

She cried out, her head against the wall, the tiles cool against her back while Xav seared the rest of her.

She felt her peak nearing, her vision blurring with the wildness Xav dragged to the surface. Her claws came out, but she sheathed them quickly, not wanting to hurt him.

"It's okay," Xav whispered. "I don't mind a little scratch."

Lindsay opened her eyes, feeling them change to Shifter, but she tamped down the beast within. The line between scratching and shredding was thin.

Xav's smile was feral. Before Lindsay could do anything more, he lifted her up and then slid inside her, fitting her perfectly onto him.

Lindsay's groan turned to a wail as Xav pulled her down onto him, bracing her against the wall while he thrust.

He was hard and big, strong. Xav's muscles worked under her fingers as she grappled with him, his skin smooth.

Lindsay sobbed his name, her mating frenzy spiking. She needed all of him, *now*, and to never stop. Never, never stop.

"I won't," Xav vowed, and Lindsay realized she'd said the words out loud. "Never, Linds. You'll never be rid of me."

"Good." Lindsay clung to him, silencing them both by taking his mouth in a hot kiss.

Xav continued his thrusts, the bathroom echoing with their groans and cries of crazed need. At least, Lindsay felt crazed. Xav closed his eyes while he loved her, then he opened them wide when he hit his climax, his seed scalding.

His smile when he slowed, the water pattering around them, was the most beautiful thing Lindsay had ever seen, and so was the love in his eyes.

———

"Tell me about the scent marking," Xav said.

They lay in his bed, their bodies still damp, even after their quick dry off with the towel. Lindsay's hair stuck out in golden clumps, which Xav thought was adorable.

They hadn't been able to keep their hands off each other as they'd made for the bedroom, leaving piles of dropped clothes and wet towels on the bathroom floor. Xav had wanted to touch Lindsay all over, and he did it as he swept her onto the bed, and then lowered himself to her again, fiercely thrusting inside her.

He'd been a long way from spent. He never would be with Lindsay.

After a time, they'd stretched out comfortably together

while they caught their breaths. Lindsay had her head on Xav's shoulder and now looked up at him quizzically.

"Your brother is mated to a Shifter," she reminded him. "You must have heard of scent marking."

"Heard the term." Xav brushed back a lock of her still-damp hair. "Don't know exactly what it means."

Lindsay laced her fingers through his, the flush on her cheek revealing her embarrassment. "There's a scent Shifters can breathe onto each other, very faint, but discernable to Shifters. Eric tried to explain to me once that there's a gland or something, but I didn't really understand, or at the time, care. It tells other Shifters to leave you alone."

Xav squeezed her hand. "You mean I smell? Can't I wash it off? We used a lot of soap in there." He grinned at the happy memory of the shower.

"No," Lindsay's flush deepened. "It's not really scent. It's more like ... a sense. Any Shifter walking by you just *knows*."

"Knows what?"

Lindsay looked up at him, her eyes holding anguish. "That you're mine."

Xav watched her in puzzlement. "Is that a bad thing?"

"No." Lindsay's answer was quick. "Unless you think it is. I can remove it. I think."

"No wonder Neal and Brody stared at me so hard when they came in yesterday. You did this last night?"

"Yes." She looked away again.

Xav put his finger under Lindsay's chin and turned her to face him. "I think it's obvious I don't mind. Tell me next time, though, okay? So I know what's going on when Shifters make fun of me about it."

"There isn't a next time. It's on you, for good. Unless I remove it. If I can." She shrugged. "Ask Eric. He's like the walking encyclopedia of Shifter information."

"It has nothing to do with the mate-claim?"

Lindsay again evaded his gaze. "No. Scent marking can lead to one but doesn't have to."

Xav studied her a moment, not liking to see her so uneasy, but he had to know about these things. "I talked to Tiger about the mate bond," he said quietly.

Lindsay stiffened. "Did you?"

You and Lindsay are two halves, Tiger had said. *Make them whole.*

Xav still wasn't sure how he was going to do that.

"Don't you want to know what he said about it?" Xav asked.

He didn't imagine Lindsay's disquiet. "Tiger's always sure everything will work out," she said. "Jinxie is too. Shifters who have the mate bond can't always imagine what it's like not to form it."

Xav's heart thumped. "Are we forming it?"

Lindsay watched him in sadness. "I don't know."

Did that mean that Lindsay didn't feel the mate bond for *him*? Cassidy had once explained a bit about it, but Lindsay was right, those who had it couldn't really convey its meaning to those who didn't.

"How can we tell?" Xav asked. "What is it supposed to feel like?"

Lindsay lightly touched his chest. "I'm not sure, actually. But if both of us don't form it, we're better off not mating at all." She drew a sharp breath. "Don't ask me to answer about the mate-claim, not right now. I have a lot to think about. 'Kay?"

"I wasn't going to." Xav lifted her fingers to his lips and pressed kisses to each fingertip. "I know it's a tough choice. I made the claim to keep the other Shifters off your back. It stays until you decide. "

Lindsay moaned and fell onto him, burying her face in his shoulder. "Why are you so sweet to me?"

Xav shrugged, tamping down his fears about his future with her. "I'm a sweet guy. Now, I can think of a few things we can do while you're thinking."

"Mm?" Lindsay said into his shoulder, sounding more like her playful self. "What things?"

Xav slid his hand under her hair and coaxed her to raise her head. He read desire in her eyes, the raw need flaring again.

"Maybe something like this." Xav rolled her over beneath him, then he licked her from neck to navel.

Lindsay squealed with laughter as he buzzed his mouth on her abdomen, then her laughter turned to a hungry moan when he trailed his tongue between her thighs to taste her.

———

XAV SWAM UPWARD FROM PROFOUND SLUMBER HOURS LATER when he heard a faint clatter in the kitchen.

His first thought was that Lindsay had risen to fix herself a snack—Shifters were always hungry—before he realized that Lindsay slept contentedly next to him.

Xav had this place well stocked with state-of-the-art security and cams, but any tech could be bypassed if someone had the know-how. He could name a few Shifters, like Neal, who did.

However, Shifters would make no noise. Therefore, the person trying to be quiet in Xav's kitchen was human.

Xav softly slid open his nightstand drawer and removed the pistol he kept there.

Lindsay instantly came awake. *Instantly.* Unlike Xav, who'd lain in sonorous confusion for a few seconds, she was up and on her feet, staring into the darkness beyond his bedroom door.

To his alarm, she motioned for him to stay put and

slipped into the hall. Lindsay was stark naked, her pale hair a smudge in the darkness. She'd removed her fake Collar sometime during their play, so not even that marred her nude body.

While Xav figured she'd stun the hell out of whoever was in his house with her wild beauty, he wouldn't sit and wait for her to be shot.

He heaved himself quietly out of bed, just as naked, and followed her.

Lindsay had already made it to the front of the house by the time Xav emerged from the bedroom. A light flared on in the kitchen, and Lindsay's voice rang out.

"Oh, boys, you're having a party without me?" Then a crash of furniture and Lindsay saying "Shi—" before she was silenced.

Xav burst into the kitchen, his pistol ready. Lindsay lay on the floor, sprawled inelegantly, a tranq dart in her shoulder. Before Xav could fire, he felt a sting in his back and a lassitude that announced he too had been tranqed.

Damn, I'm getting sick of this, was his last coherent thought before the floor rushed upward to meet him.

CHAPTER SEVENTEEN

Xav swam into and out of consciousness, each time trying to haul himself up and fight whoever had knocked him out before sinking into blackness again.

Once, he felt a rocking movement beneath him and smelled the close confines of a vehicle. Screwing open his eyes revealed that he lay in the back of a large van, with what felt like a scratchy carpet beneath him. Lindsay was curled up next to Xav, seemingly asleep, which relieved the hell of out him. They were both still unclothed, but at least the van was heated.

Moving lights reflected in the two small windows on the rear door, but Xav had no energy to pull himself up and peer through them, let alone try to break them to slither out.

When he half woke the next time, he reflected that whoever had grabbed him had done a much better job keeping him under than AC's boys. They also hadn't bound his hands or feet, which meant they weren't worried about him getting away.

While there were many enemies who possibly could have done this, Xav focused on the most likely culprit—the gang who'd nabbed Dean. They must have known Xav and Diego were investigating them, and they weren't the kind of people who'd make an appointment at DX's offices if they had questions.

They must want to know what Xav and DX Security knew —and what Jeff had told them—to decide whether DX would pose any kind of threat. Or, if they were trying to reel in AC, maybe they wanted more bait.

They need Xav and Lindsay alive, Xav concluded, before he slid into unconsciousness again. Or else they'd have simply killed them both—or tried to, anyway.

The next time Xav came to, his head was much clearer, though his mouth was parchment dry, and he had a foul taste in his throat.

He was no longer in the van but lying on a cold cement floor in a place that felt large, with a pile of fabric on top of him. He fumbled at the fabric and discovered it was clothes— jeans and a sweatshirt. His own, in fact.

While it was dark in here, it wasn't pitch black. Light filtered in from somewhere, showing him a tall aisle with filled shelves in what looked like a large warehouse. Lindsay was nowhere in sight.

Xav went cold with fear, but incandescent rage quickly followed.

If they'd touched Lindsay, or even looked at her, *his mate*, they would pay with all the blood in their bodies.

Xav quickly slid into the garments, having to stop from time to time as dizziness took over. His captors hadn't bothered to grab underwear, socks, or shoes, he thought in annoyance, but at least they were letting him cover his ass.

Once Xav was dressed and no longer felt like he was about to puke, he leveraged himself to his feet. He wasn't guarded, which again, did not bode well. His abductors believed he couldn't get away and that he posed no threat.

They were wrong, of course, but Xav would let them think what they wanted.

There was no question this time of Diego tracking Xav. The tracker he'd worn for the mission was back home, along with his phone and the rest of his life. Xav had only this sweatshirt and jeans with empty pockets.

He had an entire warehouse of who knew what goodies that might help him, but first Xav needed to find Lindsay.

He started down the long aisle toward what looked like open space at its end. He had to pause and hang onto shelves to keep upright at first, but as his muscles uncramped and blood flowed, the effects of the drug lessened.

While the floor was cold to his bare feet, it wasn't freezing. Xav would welcome coolness like this in the middle of the blistering summer.

The shelves were filled with unmarked boxes, many dusty. Xav wondered if this place had been abandoned by whatever company had stored their stuff here, and the gang had simply appropriated it.

Once he emerged from the aisle, Xav found himself in the corner of a vast warehouse with many more aisles of shelves and pallets of crates across the floor. Moonlight filtered through high ventilation windows, and a warmer light filled the windows of a walled office space that had been built in the center of the large room.

Xav kept to the shadows as he approached the office, then he pressed himself against a solid part of its wall and carefully peered through a bent slat in one of the windows' blinds.

The small workspace inside was devoid of the desks, worktables, or shelving found in most offices. It held a few swivel chairs, like those a person would use at a computer station, plus a long folding table against one wall that held a microwave and a coffee maker.

Lindsay sat on one of the swivel chairs. They hadn't bound her, and she lounged with her legs folded up under her.

She wore the cargo pants and the thin fleece shirt she'd donned to hike around the desert in, but no shoes or jacket. She was wide awake, Xav could see, and far less groggy than Xav still felt.

The three men in the room with Lindsay showed no wariness of her at all. They had no weapon trained on her and weren't watching her that closely. No worries that she'd attack them, slash them with claws, and easily race away.

Xav felt a grin pull at his face. They didn't realize Lindsay was Shifter.

She's left her fake Collar on his nightstand, and even if she'd not shed it, they might not have recognized it if they weren't familiar with Shifters. She bore a thin scar where the real Collar had once fused into her skin, but again, if these humans didn't realize what that meant, they'd pay it no attention.

Xav studied the three with her. The two standing were obvious bone-breakers, hired for their muscle and ruthlessness. The dark-haired man with hard blue eyes, who sat in a swivel chair facing Lindsay, was clearly in charge.

He was younger than the other two, thirties at most. Xav had never seen him before, but his features were familiar, probably because he looked a lot like the AC of fifteen years ago.

Apparently, they'd found Dean.

He sat upright in the chair without being stiff, the man full of confidence and at his ease. He didn't look like a captive, even one who'd decided to fall in with his captors. People who'd joined criminals after they'd been taken by them usually wore an air of defiance, as though daring anyone to dispute their choice.

Dean regarded Lindsay as though trying to decide if she'd be an asset or a vulnerability. If the latter, Xav feared, he'd dispose of her.

Lindsay never turned her head or came alert when Xav peeked into the room, but Xav knew she sensed him there. He couldn't say why, but he felt her presence so tangibly she might have been pressed against him. There was a tingle in his chest, one that warmed when he looked at her.

"Are you going to kill us?" Lindsay's voice held the perfect amount of shakiness. "Can I call my mom and tell her goodbye?"

"You aren't calling anyone, sweetie," Dean answered without rancor. "We're waiting for your boyfriend to wake up and join us. Once he does, we'll talk about what happens to you. I have a lot of questions for him."

Lindsay's mouth drooped. "You are going to kill us. Why? I never did anything to you."

Xav wanted to warn her not to lay it on so thick, but he could only watch and listen.

"I know *you* didn't," Dean answered. "But Xavier and his brother are getting in my way. They've teamed up with *my* brother, who has become a serious pain in my ass."

"Your brother's worried about you," Lindsay offered.

"Sure, he is." Dean chuckled, a chilling sound. "He's worried he won't get a piece of the money I've been smart enough to make. He's a washed-up loser. There's a reason I don't want him anywhere near me."

Of course. Xav knew AC had been lying all along, though he hadn't been certain exactly about what. Dean might have originally joined up with this gang against his will, but it looked like he'd long ago thrown off his shackles and gladly risen through its ranks.

AC had probably heard how Dean had orchestrated the robbery from the money launderers, and planned for his own payout. AC had grabbed Xav, who was close to his own brother, and recruited Shifters, who were all about family, telling them the pathetic tale of wanting to reunite with Dean. He'd used Lindsay's soft heart against her.

Lindsay realized this at the same time, because her pathetic pose evaporated. "You mean he played me?" she asked, voice rising in anger. "That son of a bitch."

"You aren't the first to be duped by my brother, honey," Dean said. "He's shit on me most of my life. The day he was carted off to prison was the happiest day I could remember. I wanted to thank the Escobars for putting him away, but now I want to shoot them for almost leading him to me."

"Is that why you were helicoptering all over the desert?" Lindsay asked, as though merely curious. "To keep AC from finding you?"

Dean shook his head. "No, no, to look for good stashing places. When you acquire a lot of cash, people want to take it from you. I was hunting for a place to put it for safekeeping. All those old silver mines are great for hiding things in."

"Did you find one?" Lindsay's question held the eagerness of a woman dazzled by the thought of loads of loot.

Dean laughed. "If I had, I wouldn't tell you, but no. The places we explored were too dangerous. It doesn't help to leave your money somewhere that will cave in as soon as it rains hard enough. The mines can be useful for other things, though."

Like disposing of bodies, Xav mused. His and Lindsay's maybe.

Xav decided to come off the sidelines. He readied himself for a fight but strolled casually into the room, treading carefully on his bare feet.

"You okay, Linds?" he asked before acknowledging Dean's presence.

"Yeah." Lindsay's expression became that of a scared

woman worried about herself and her boyfriend. He saw the flicker of Shifter impatience in her eyes, but she hid it heroically. "You?"

"Fine." Xav turned to Dean. "I guess we found you."

"No, my man, I found *you*." Dean grinned. "I had my guys track down who the hell was dogging us. I'd never heard of DX Security, but when I looked into it, I realized that Xavier and Diego Escobar had turned into hired guns. Respect."

Xav shrugged. "It's a living."

Dean lost his smile, his face hardening. "Then I found out you were working for AC, my scummy brother. I couldn't believe it. You put him away, now you're *helping* him? He was coming after me and my money, you idiot."

Xav opened his hands. "What can I say? He appealed to our better natures, and we felt sorry for him. We had no idea of his true motives. So, why break into my house and take me and Lindsay? Leverage to make Diego throw AC to the wolves?"

"I only meant to grab *you*, Escobar. We didn't realize you'd brought your girlfriend home for some celebration. She saw my guys, so they brought her along."

Xav lounged against the wall near the door, a vantage point from which he could assess the situation and decide what to do. He'd been well and truly tranqued on the drive here, so he had no idea how far they'd come. Might have been two hours, might have been two days. They could be just outside Las Vegas or two states away. Likely still in the southwestern deserts though, or it would be colder in the unheated warehouse.

"What do you want me to do?" Xav asked as though unworried. "Tell Diego we were duped and to send AC back to jail? Give me a phone, and I'll make the call." He stretched out a hand.

Dean scowled. "What I want is my brother dead and out

of my life. You're going to help me make that happen, Escobar. Your girlfriend here can be my leverage over you. If I like what you do, I'll send you two off to Tahiti or somewhere you can have a great long vacation. If I don't ..." Dean gestured to the thug on his right. "Your girlfriend is shot and killed while you watch."

"That's not fair," Lindsay said at once. "I can help you as much as Xav can."

Dean's eyebrows rose, his sourness falling away. "Ooh, she's ballsy. Don't worry, sweetheart. If you're right, I'll give you a job. No matter what, though—if either of you disobeys me, the other is dead."

Lindsay instantly became contrite. "Can I at least call my mom? She'll be worried sick. I'll tell her I'm all right, and that's it. Promise." She made her voice grow thick with tears.

"Sorry, babe. No phone calls. When you're on your way to Tahiti, then you can call home."

Lindsay scrunched up her face, as though preventing herself from crying. "Can I at least go to the bathroom? I really have to pee." She unfolded herself, letting her lithe movements distract the standing thugs.

Dean jerked his chin at one of his henchmen. "Take her. Stand outside the door, but break it down if she stays in there too long." He frowned at Lindsay, unimpressed with her beauty. "Don't do anything cute, or your lover gets it in the back of the head."

Lindsay flinched and nodded, as though frightened.

The henchman led her out, Lindsay brushing past Xav, who remained in place.

Xav laid a hand on her shoulder as she passed. "Stay strong, baby," he said in a low voice.

Lindsay leaned into his touch, as though she couldn't help herself, then gave him a wan smile and let the goon herd her out.

Xav had no idea what she was planning, but he steeled himself for whatever it might be.

Dean turned to Xav once Lindsay was gone. He hadn't left his seat, comfortable in his authority.

"Nice lady you found," he said. "Again, respect."

Xav had no intention of discussing Lindsay's finer points with him. "Tahiti, my ass," he said easily. "When you're done with us, you'll dump our bodies into one of those convenient hidden mine shafts."

Dean shrugged, unconcerned. "We'll see."

"You'll have to get hold of another helicopter if you want to do that. The one you left in Death Valley is toast."

"Yeah, our pilot said there was a defect in the electrical system or something. That was scary shit, riding it down, but we made it. He's busy negotiating for another copter." A smile touched Dean's mouth at Xav's surprised expression. "Did you think I'd kill him for crashing our ride? It wasn't his fault, and it's hard to find a dependable pilot."

Jeff almost hadn't made it, Xav reminded himself. Dean had left a broken man behind to die.

"That's true," Xav agreed, keeping his anger under control. "I know a pilot who refuses to work for anyone but himself. I've offered him permanent employment, but he prefers to freelance. Likes his space."

"Pilots are their own breed." Dean's eyes narrowed. "You're smart, Escobar. Capable. I could use you in my organization."

"We'll see." Xav shrugged, mimicking Dean's words. "Is that why you brought me here? To offer me a job?"

"No." Dean's lips twitched. "I told you, you're going to bring my brother in. And then you're going to execute him for me."

CHAPTER EIGHTEEN

L indsay remained docile as the henchman walked her to a pair of doors not far from the office and gestured to the one marked *Ladies*.

"Don't lock it behind you," he commanded. "You have five minutes, and then I'm coming in."

"There are some businesses that can't be rushed," Lindsay told him with a smile. "But don't worry. I don't want your big boss in there to hurt my guy."

"Wise." The man opened the door. It was a regular door, not a push open, like in a public restroom, and the doorknob had a lock. Beyond was a single room with no windows that held a toilet, a sink, and a shelf with a mirror so its occupant could primp before returning to work.

Lindsay scuttled inside without thanking him—why should she?—and pointedly waited for him to close the door.

She turned on the sink's faucet to cover any noise she might make, pleased that it had good flow, not a trickle. Then she made her way to the toilet, because she really did have to pee.

Once she finished and washed up, with the toilet flush

further disguising sound, Lindsay pulled out the cell phone she'd lifted from the thug as he'd walked her out here. Her biggest worry was that he'd get bored and try to check his messages or scroll social media, but a look at the phone told her there was no Wi-Fi connection and only a weak phone signal.

She opened the text function, input a number she knew by heart, typed her brief but coded message, sent it, and deleted the text.

Lindsay pocketed the phone and was out of the bathroom with a minute and a half to spare.

"All done," she said sweetly.

The thug, whose face hadn't softened one iota, seized her by the arm to propel her back to the office. Lindsay suppressed her lynx's instinct to throw him across the floor and used the opportunity to slide his phone quietly back into his pocket.

When they reached the office, she sent Xav a reassuring smile and resumed her seat.

"Dean was just saying he wants me to bring AC to him and kill him myself," Xav told her. "Probably so he won't be charged with AC's murder. He hasn't explained how I'm supposed to do that when I don't even know where I am."

"You'll have AC taken to the location I've already picked," Dean said with exaggerated patience. "You'll ride there with me. Your girlfriend will remain here as a guarantee you won't try to get away, deceive me, or otherwise cause damage. I've already described what will happen if you mess with me."

"I suppose all I have to do is tell Diego I've found you," Xav said, as though logistics were his only concern. "And have him bring AC to a meetup. Diego won't come alone, though. He'll bring serious backup."

"I'd expect him to," Dean acknowledged. "Doesn't matter. I really don't give a rat's ass. I might have hired you to find AC in the first place if I'd known about you and that he was stalking me. Bring me AC, go the hell home, or on your vacation in Tahiti. I don't care. You just need to make sure your bro doesn't help AC try to kill *me*."

"I will, but this means I *do* have to call Diego," Xav pointed out.

"Yep." Dean nodded. "We'll get to that."

Xav had edged closer to Lindsay's chair during the conversation. He seemed calm and resigned, but Lindsay scented his tension. He was readying himself to fight.

She wanted to tell him he only needed to stall, but she couldn't say anything with Dean and his two goons keeping their beady eyes on them both.

Lindsay reached for the mate bond inside her and sent her thoughts to Xav. This would only work if he was also forming the bond, but might not even then. Xav couldn't read her mind, only understand the gist of what she was trying to convey.

Xav stiffened the slightest bit, and Lindsay's heart thumped. Had he felt that?

His smoldering glance at her told her he did.

Lindsay subsided, her body flushing with joy and inconvenient rising mate frenzy coupled with vast relief. The doubts that had made her nearly ill the last few days—no, since she'd met Xav in the first place—receded before a rush of exhilaration. With that came even more mating need.

Good thing these guys weren't Shifters, because Lindsay would have just given herself away big time.

"I'm not even sure what time it is," Xav was saying to Dean. "But if I call Diego in the middle of the night, bouncing him out of bed with news that I found you, he'll be very suspicious. He sent me home to enjoy time with my girlfriend, not continue the hunt."

Dean didn't seem impressed. "We have a couple of hours

before we start. By the time we reach where I want to go, it will be a reasonable time of day. He'll believe you."

It was likely that Dean wanted to go back out to the area around Death Valley, Lindsay reasoned behind the blur of her Shifter euphoria. He could bury AC's body in a mine shaft or in a crevice in its badlands. He might try to bury Xav there too.

Not this Shifter's mate, Lindsay vowed silently. Dean Parkes had messed with the wrong girl.

"What kind of warehouse was this?" Lindsay asked him genially, as though the discussion didn't interest her. "They have any shoes?" She pointed her bare toe. "My feet are cold."

Dean studied her a moment, while Lindsay kept herself from springing at him and ripping his face off. She had to wait, to find out how many people were actually in and around the warehouse, and to make her move when she was certain Xav would be safe.

For now, she pretended to be the slightly dim girlfriend of the hot Xav, not quite sure what she'd gotten herself into. The kind of woman who wasn't a danger to the big bad criminals.

Both thugs watched her closely, but they took their cues from Dean. To think, Lindsay had pictured him as a scared, anguished victim of the gang that had imprisoned him.

That the cruel leader Jeff had mentioned was Dean himself explained Jeff's slight confusion when they'd asked if Dean had escaped the crash. Also his sudden impulse to run, if he'd thought they were either working for Dean or out to kill the man and his gang. And, while AC clearly hadn't known Jeff, Jeff had likely seen the strong resemblance between him and Dean and concluded who he was.

Dean looked Lindsay over thoughtfully, but she could tell he came from a world where women were either used or dismissed. Xav said nothing at all, only watched and waited, the connection Lindsay had felt strengthening with every heartbeat.

"I don't know what all the hell is out there," Dean said to her. "Explore. Have fun. I need to talk Xav anyway."

"She does like her shoes," Xav said with a touch of amusement.

Dean gave a curt nod to the thug who'd escorted Lindsay to the bathroom. "Watch her. Keep in touch."

The henchmen acknowledged this and gestured Lindsay to the door. Lindsay skirted Dean, taking her time, sending him a coy glance as she went around him. Then she did a finger wave at the three men as she scooted out with the guard.

"Wow, a whole warehouse," Lindsay said loudly once they were clear of the office. "Free shopping."

She sashayed toward an aisle lined with tall shelving, pretending to scan them. Now to put her plans into motion and hope that her message had been received.

———

DIEGO JERKED OUT OF SLEEP NEXT TO CASSIDY, WHO'D COME awake and alert with Shifter speed. Someone was pounding on the back door of the house, beating on it without remorse.

Cassidy skimmed out of bed with the grace of her cat, heading down the hall while Diego was still untangling himself from covers. She didn't bother with a robe, but ran in her thin sleep shirt, which she could easily throw off to shift if necessary.

Eric was already at the back door by the time Diego, weapon in hand, reached it a few steps behind Cassidy. Diego didn't push in front of his mate, because he knew Cassidy wouldn't let him, plus she could strike faster if he wasn't in her way.

Both Eric and Cassidy relaxed at the same time, which told Diego that whoever was outside wasn't dangerous. Eric opened the door.

Leah Cummings stood on the doorstep, a bleary-eyed Martin behind her.

"You have to help Lindsay," Leah said in a rush, her voice holding near hysteria. "Round up Shiftertown. Let's go."

Diego came alert once more. "Where is she? Is she with Xav?"

"I don't know," Leah snapped in frustration. "*Find* her."

"Stop." Eric's low but commanding tone made Leah draw a long, shaking breath. "Talk to me, Leah. How do you know she's in trouble?"

"Because she sent me *this*." Leah thrust a small, old-model cell phone into Eric's face so he could see the message on it.

Diego peered over Eric's shoulder, as did Cassidy, her fragrant hair touching Diego's nose.

The text beneath a ten-digit number Diego didn't recognize read *XO*.

When Diego had been a kid, Xs had meant kisses, Os hugs. Girls would write them on notes, and his mom had used them sometimes when she was feeling whimsical.

Diego wondered if the letters meant something different to Shifters, but Eric looked baffled. "I don't understand."

Leah jerked the cell phone back. "It's Lindsay's way of telling us she's in trouble. We taught her that as a cub when we lived in the Yukon. She could sketch it on a tree in the woods or on a street in a town, and we'd know she needed help. We've kept it as our family SOS ever since." Leah gazed at Eric pleadingly. "She wouldn't send it if it wasn't serious. You're her leader. *Lead*."

"Diego, where's Xav?" Eric asked.

Diego had been texting Xav before Leah finished her

explanation, but with no response. He put through a call to hear a few rings before it rolled to voicemail.

This is Xav. Leave a message.

Xav's work-only cell phone did the same thing.

Lindsay was the most capable woman Diego had ever met, apart from Cassidy, and he knew she wouldn't ask for help lightly. If Xav couldn't assist her, that meant Xav was in trouble as well.

"Let me see the text again," Diego asked Leah gently.

Leah willingly handed over the phone. "Can you trace her by the number she used?"

"*I* can't," Diego said. "But I know someone who can." He touched another contact on his own phone, this one for Neal, who answered with his wolf's growl. Diego explained the situation, and Neal's snarls increased.

"There's only a baby computer up here," Neal said, whatever that meant. "But I'll give it a shot. AC's asleep. At least *someone* is relaxing. I'll keep you posted."

He signed off without a goodbye, but Diego knew Neal well enough now to understand that his abruptness meant he was troubled.

"I'll start at Xav's house," Diego announced. "That's where he was heading when I last saw him, eight hours ago."

"Good." Leah turned away. "Let's go."

"Leah." Eric called after her. "We have to think about this first. Pinpoint where she'd most likely be instead of running around over the entire state."

Leah swung back. "We do what Diego says and go to Xav's. If she was there, I can find her scent and track her."

"It might be more complicated than that," Eric tried.

Leah glared at him. "I think I can track my *own daughter.* Come on. Let's do this." She marched away, Martin following her with the same grim determination.

"I'll take them, Eric," Diego said, hoping Leah would at

least give him a few seconds to dress. "Round up who you need to. Iona, I think *you* should have the job of waking up Tiger. He's less likely to rip you to shreds."

Iona sent him an amused nod. "I'm on it." Tiger and Carly, with Seth, were staying with Graham, whose large house could accommodate guests. Not that Graham had complied docilely with Eric's request to let Tiger in.

Eric scowled. "Hey, since everyone else knows what to do, maybe I'll go back to bed."

"No, you won't," Diego said as he started down the hall to his and Cassidy's bedroom. "Meet up with us at Xav's. We'll use it as a base. Keep the bigger Shifters out of sight, though, so his neighbors don't freak out and call Shifter Bureau."

"I can do my job, Escobar." When Eric used Diego's surname, Diego knew he was on the edge of losing his leopard temper.

"Good," was all Diego said. "See you there."

Diego reached the bedroom and pulled on clothes he always kept ready for emergencies. Cassidy had followed him and dressed even more quickly.

"I'm coming with you," she announced as Diego did up his belt.

"Cass ..."

"Lindsay is my best friend," Cassidy said in a hard voice. "I can track her almost as well as Leah can. Iona will be here to look after Amanda."

Diego gazed into the beautiful eyes he loved, and relented. He knew she was right, and he missed working with Cassidy by his side.

He leaned forward and softly kissed her lips. "Let's go then, *querida*."

Cassidy bathed him in her warm smile and proceeded him out the door.

Not until they had driven halfway to Xav's, Leah and

Martin sitting firmly together in the back seat, did Diego realize they had stowaways.

"Is this another adventure, Uncle Diego?" a little boy asked from the very back of the SUV.

"Don't worry," his identical twin brother said to Leah and Martin, who didn't seem as startled as Diego was. "We'll find Lindsay. Lindsay's nice."

It was far too late to turn around and drive them back to Shiftertown. Diego sighed, hoping Graham wouldn't kill him for taking Matt and Kyle once more into danger.

———

"THESE ARE CUTE." LINDSAY HELD UP A PAIR OF SNEAKERS IN delight. She'd dug them from a mountain of Styrofoam peanuts in a box she'd asked the henchman to lift down from an upper shelf for her. The shoes were years out of date but crisply new from whatever factory had made them, bright blue and studded with sparkling stones. She waved them at her watcher. "Don't you think these are cute?"

The man slapped dust from the box off his hands and shrugged. "They aren't bad."

"You should scrounge some for your girlfriend," Lindsay suggested. "Or your sister, or mom." She winked. "Get on their good side."

"Maybe."

At least the guy was talking to her. He'd gone from silent menace to halfway human during Lindsay's jabbering, lowering his guard.

"Ooh, I should try on some of these shirts." Lindsay beamed as she lifted a pink and gray T-shirt from another box he'd heaved down. "But then, I'd have to take this one off." She plucked at her loose sweatshirt, which had been easy to shuck for shifting. "Would you like to see that?"

The man started, but his guard went down even further. "I guess I wouldn't mind."

"While the boys shut us out, we should have some fun." Lindsay danced down the aisle, deeper into shadow. "You stay right there." She pointed a forefinger at him. "And I'll put on a show."

The man didn't seem surprised by this offer, but if he lived in Las Vegas, he might think Lindsay was a dancer at one of the burlesque clubs, used to baring herself. Some Shifter women did work at the clubs, and the men too, as Shifters saw no shame in showing their bodies. *If you've got it, flaunt it,* they said.

Lindsay had no shame about her body either, and this man would have already seen it if he'd helped his fellow goons drag her and Xav to the van or into the warehouse. But the way he glued his gaze to her was creepy. If Lindsay could figure out another way to quickly get out of her clothes to shift, she'd take it.

The man leaned against a stack of boxes, relaxing, as Lindsay turned her back and shimmied off her sweatshirt, twirling it around before tossing it away. She had no bra or underwear on, because they hadn't been nice enough to bring them along when they'd kidnapped her.

Next, she slipped off her pants, which left her completely bare-assed.

Lindsay didn't give the guy time to have much of a show. She darted around the end of the shelves into darkness, laughing as though teasing him, daring him to follow.

Her heart beat wildly as she started the shift, but thankfully, it came a little faster tonight. The Shifter in her must know Lindsay needed to be in the form that gave her the most advantage.

"Hey," came a shout behind her. "Where'd you go?"

She heard his footsteps around the corner, but by the

time her guard reached the dark end of the aisle, Lindsay had sprung high on her lynx paws, noiselessly making it to the top of the shelves.

The man halted in bewilderment, but Lindsay didn't stay to gloat. She sprinted across the tops of the shelves, putting her plans into motion.

CHAPTER NINETEEN

Diego's rage rose as he and Cassidy searched Xav's new home, finding scattered clothing, rifled drawers, and the shoes Xav liked to wear waiting by the bed for him to slip them on.

The wolf cubs scampered here, there, and everywhere, noses busily taking in scents, tails wagging hard.

Only Cassidy, Tiger, the cubs, and Leah had entered the house with Diego. The rest of the Shifters, with a contingent of DX men and Emma, waited down the street and around the corner. Diego had wanted to keep Tiger out of sight, but he'd weighed the possibility of the neighbors being spooked against Tiger's unique tracking abilities and decided to risk it.

Leah uttered a cry as she snatched up Lindsay's jacket from the living room rug. She buried her face in it, but she didn't weep, as though trying to stay strong.

Tiger stood in the middle of the kitchen, eyes closed. This was his way of assessing a situation, Carly had once tried to explain, though Diego hadn't really understood. Tiger could sense things, apparently, that other Shifters could not.

A super-Shifter, they called him. Tiger would sometimes don a cape to amuse the cubs, who adored him.

Matt and Kyle scrambled up Tiger's motionless body without fear, perching on his shoulders while they waited for him to figure things out.

Tiger opened his eyes, which were yellow-gold and intense.

"There were four captors inside the house," he announced. "They used tranquilizers, most likely in darts, to subdue Xavier and Lindsay. From the residue, the tranq was strong enough to put a human out for a few hours, but a Shifter for only half that long." Tiger met Diego's incredulous expression with a deadpan one. "I learned much about tranquilizers."

From the scientists who'd experimented on him, Diego knew Tiger meant. They'd tested all kinds of drugs on him, gauging his reaction to them and building up his resistance.

"Interesting," Diego said, tamping down his disquiet. "Why didn't they give Lindsay a stronger dose?"

"Because they didn't realize she's Shifter," Leah said, triumphant, as she emerged from the bedroom. She held out a Collar, one of the fakes Eric and Liam Morrissey had created. "She fooled them. *And* she got hold of a phone." She radiated pride in her daughter.

"Lindsay's not dim," Cassidy agreed with enthusiasm.

Of course, who the captors were and why they'd taken both Xav and Lindsay remained a mystery. The most logical solution was that the gang they'd been tailing had decided to find out who'd been following them, and why. Jeff was being guarded, but he might have managed to report in to his leader—if Jeff still felt any loyalty to him—and tell them about DX Security.

Diego's phone buzzed. His heart leapt in hope that it would be Xav responding, but the readout said it was Neal.

"What did you find?" Diego asked him.

"A name." Neal's wolf rumbles came over the line. "I was able to hack into the guy's number and pull up his calls and texts. He's called Ron Becker. Lives off Harmon, near Sam's Town."

"He sounds familiar. Wait a sec." Diego seated himself at Xav's computer, which the kidnappers had also left intact, and logged into DX Security, scouring its records. "Shit."

Diego sat back as the screen showed him its information on Ron Becker.

"What?" Cassidy leaned over him, her silken hair brushing his cheek.

"He used to work for AC Parkes," Diego announced. "Neal —grab AC, drag him down here, and meet us at DX Security. He's going to tell us *everything* he knows and where Xav and Lindsay are most likely to be."

———

DEAN REACHED INTO A POCKET, AND XAV TENSED BEFORE THE man slid out a cell phone. "While your girlfriend is enjoying herself, you can call your brother."

Xav raised his brows. "I thought we were waiting for a reasonable hour."

Dean shrugged. "I changed my mind. Have him fetch AC, and then we'll give him another call when we get to the location and tell him an exact meeting point."

"If I phone Diego from an unknown number, he either won't answer, or won't believe I haven't been coerced," Xav argued.

"Maybe." Dean caressed the cell phone's black face with his thumb. "But this is *my* number, which he can verify. He'll believe that you found me."

"Even so, Diego will be snuggled in bed with his lady. He won't want to answer a call from anyone."

"Be persistent."

"All right." Xav heaved a sigh as he reached for the phone. "I'll put up with Diego reaming me out, if he even answers."

Dean set the phone on the table next to the coffee maker and stepped away from it. He wasn't going to let Xav come too close. "Convince him you've found me, tell him to fetch my brother, and say you'll bring him to a location you'll fix later. Pretend you're being extra cautious about my enemies catching us."

"And then I take my girl to Tahiti?" Xav asked with feigned ingenuousness. "I'll need to grab my passport."

"We'll talk about that once I see my brother."

Xav didn't think much of AC's chances of getting out of this alive, or his own, or Lindsay's, or Diego's either. Xav's advantage was that Diego wasn't stupid and had much experience saving Xav's butt. Plus Xav had Lindsay and whatever wild ideas were in her head.

Xav took a step to the table and reached for the phone.

The lights went out.

The room didn't go completely dark, because emergency lights above the door instantly glowed. That was too bad, because Xav couldn't use cover of darkness to grab the phone or tackle his captors.

The remaining henchman drew his firearm. "What the fuck?"

Dean calmly opened a blind and peered through the office window. "Whole building is down." He didn't sound concerned.

"You hooked up to the grid out here?" Xav asked. "Or is it all generators?"

Dean shot him a derisive look, not about to tell him

whether they were within a city's power supply. "It goes off sometimes. This whole place needs work."

"Probably abandoned for a reason," Xav said, as though he commiserated.

"Probably." Dean gave his guard a nod. "Check in with Ron."

The man pulled out a handheld radio and clicked it to talk. "Anything going on? Ron, you there?"

When there was no response, Dean at last came alert.

The henchman was about to repeat his question when static sizzled on the walkie, and Lindsay's voice came to them.

"Ron fell over in the dark," she announced. "Looks like he's hurt."

Dean scowled, but motioned to his goon. "Go check it out. Round up Jack and Kurt."

"You going to be okay in here, boss?" the man asked, glancing at Xav.

"Escobar is cool," Dean said. "Right? If he doesn't want his girlfriend to be toast."

"Should I shoot her?" the henchman asked with chilling indifference.

"Nah," Dean answered with the same detachment. "I like her. I might kill Escobar but keep her. Just make sure she behaves."

"Sure." The henchman was skeptical, but he holstered his weapon and obediently marched out.

"Let's get back to calling your brother." Dean gestured to the phone. "Keep it simple. You found me, you need to meet. He brings AC, and we all have a family reunion."

"Right." Xav kept his expression neutral as he picked up the phone.

Whatever had happened to Ron out there was Lindsay's doing, and so was the power cut. Xav knew that like he knew his own name.

You go, sweetheart.

He remembered her leaping down from on high at the stadium to wipe out the arms dealer who'd been about to shoot him. Xav wanted to laugh. Dean's guys would not know what hit them.

At the same time, Xav couldn't dial back his anxiousness about her. A gun might go off and wound Lindsay, or they might bring out the tranq darts again. He could only pray she was too fast and too tricky for Dean's men.

Dean shot Xav a hard look when he began to tap in Diego's number. "Keep it simple. No extra words, no coded messages. Got it?"

"Hey, what's between you and AC is your business," Xav said without heat. "I'll deliver him and whatever, and then I'm gone. *With* my brother, and Lindsay."

Dean gave his uncaring shrug. "We'll see how it goes."

Keeping his expression neutral, Xav tapped the last number and listened to the phone ring on the other side.

"Hey, bro," he said rapidly when Diego answered with, *Who the hell is this?* "I found Dean. This is his phone. Grab AC. I'll text you a meetup point when we get there. See you soon." He pressed the Off button as Diego began to splutter questions. "Good?" Xav asked Dean.

"Guess so," Dean said.

Xav nodded, laying down the phone, waiting for his moment to take Dean, find Lindsay, and get the hell out of there.

———

Lindsay lay on top of the tall shelving unit in lynx form once more—she'd shifted enough to answer Ron's walkie-talkie before turning it off, placing it carefully next to her, and melding back into her cat.

The second man who'd been in Dean's office came striding out, obviously looking for Ron. He found him easily enough, sprawled on his back at the base of the shelves, where Lindsay had left him.

"Shit." The man bent over his colleague, lightly shaking him. "Ron. You okay?"

He never heard Lindsay coming. She dropped from the shelves and landed on him in complete silence, toppling him to the ground. One paw pressed his face into the floor while Lindsay let the other become a hand long enough to grab the taser from his belt.

Before the man could drag in a startled breath to yell, she jammed the taser to his shoulder and stunned him. Maybe weapons *did* have their uses.

Because Lindsay had been holding him down, she couldn't avoid receiving part of the shock but jumped away fast enough that she only singed her fur. Stifling a growl, she rose into her half-human, half-beast form.

Lindsay powered off the taser so it could recharge, held it between her wildcat teeth as she became all lynx, and swarmed up the shelves to her hiding place once more, making sure not to dislodge any boxes as she went.

Later she'd have a good rummage through the crates, to see if there were any more decent shoes. They shouldn't go to waste gathering dust in this old place.

But first she needed to save her mate. Dean was danger-ous, in a calm, cold way, uncaring about what happened to anyone he left in his wake. She knew he had no intention of letting her and Xav go, no matter what he offered.

Lindsay laid the taser next to Ron's walkie and cell phone she'd relieved him of. Once she eliminated the rest of the guards, she'd figure out where this warehouse was located and call her mom again.

Scouting from above, Lindsay pinpointed more of Dean's

men. Dean had them patrolling all four corners of the warehouse, walking through their areas then meeting up in the middle to give one another the all's well signal, before they returned to wandering the aisles.

None of them hurried to see how Ron was doing or to help their colleague with him, so they must think the second guy had it covered. Or, they didn't care. A hurt man was someone else's problem.

Lindsay reasoned that there must be more guards outside, but she'd tackle them later. The men inside had been only slightly spooked by the lights going out, but they'd quickly recovered. Overloaded circuits might be a frequent occurrence.

Flying boxes weren't, though.

Lindsay grinned ferociously as she hovered above one of the guards, then flung a heavy box down at him. He heard it at the last minute, yelping and jumping aside as the box burst open in a cloud of foam peanuts.

He jerked around, weapon drawn, trying to figure out where the attack had come from, but Lindsay was already gone.

She wanted to laugh out loud, or yowl in glee, but she controlled herself. She landed on the next set of shelves and sent a whole shower of boxes cascading down, then was four aisles over by the time the slower humans reacted.

Their shouts drew the others. Lindsay bombarded all of them, scampering away before they saw her.

Lindsay leapt and caught the nearest beam, easily lifting herself onto it. The rafters that held up the vast roof were interspersed with pipes of a sprinkler system that crisscrossed the entire building. Lindsay clung to her beam and used her between-beast strength to break one of the slenderer pipes.

Nothing happened.

Damn. Lindsay glared at the dangling pipe. She reasoned the building must connected to a water supply, because she'd used the bathroom without a problem, and they'd have to have water for their coffee maker. But maybe Dean's men hadn't bothered with the flow that led to the fire suppressant system.

Well, she'd just have to find the water controls and turn it back on.

Lindsay quietly broke a few more pipes, then skimmed across the rafters to a high window. The window was narrow, used only for ventilation, but lynxes were fairly small, even Shifter ones.

Before she could slide through, however, the office door abruptly opened. Dean pushed Xav in front of him as they emerged, wedging a pistol firmly against Xav's neck.

CHAPTER TWENTY

Xav quickly scanned the warehouse when he stepped out of the doorway, but he saw only shadows playing on the lines of shelving and clusters of crates. Without moving his head, he glanced upward, taking in the few broken pipes that hung precariously from the ceiling.

"Check in," Dean bellowed into the echoing room, not about to release Xav long enough to use a walkie or phone. "I want to see everyone, front and center."

"If anything's happened to Lindsay, you're answering for it," Xav informed Dean tightly.

"Shut up." Dean dug the pistol harder into Xav's neck. "You'd better hope my boys are all right. Is your brother doing this? How did you tell him where we were?"

"I didn't," Xav said truthfully. "I didn't have time."

Xav knew damn well Diego had nothing to do with the eerie darkness and silence in the warehouse. Lindsay was out there, her wild self doing whatever the hell she wanted. He'd laugh if he wasn't so worried about her.

Xav knew that if Dean's original intention had been to kill Xav and Lindsay, he'd have done it the minute Xav had called and summoned Diego. Dean could guide Diego the rest of the way by himself, no longer needing Xav. Plus, he'd never have let Lindsay wander the warehouse with only one man to guard her.

Dean had considered Xav and Lindsay a sideshow, small potatoes. His goal was to confront his brother, AC, and he didn't give a shit about Xav and his perky girlfriend. Whether they lived or died hadn't been important.

Now, Dean was getting rattled. A power cut could be explained by faulty electrics in an old building, but things banging around and his guards yelling was a different story.

Dean pushed Xav forward, making for a small door next to large rolling ones that Xav assumed led either outside or to a loading bay. All the doors were shut tight, he saw as they approached, the small one with a padlocked bolt in place.

"No one came in that way," Xav observed. "There must be other entrances. This place has fire doors, right?"

"Check in," Dean yelled again, ignoring Xav. "If it's you, Diego Escobar, show your face, or your brother gets it in the head."

There was only silence, broken by a muffled groan from the depths of one aisle.

"Diego's not here," Xav said. "He can't answer you."

Again, Dean ignored him and kept up his conversation with the imaginary Diego. Obviously he didn't consider Lindsay capable of doing any damage, more fool he.

"I only want AC," Dean said loudly as he pushed Xav toward the aisle from which they'd heard the sound. "I'll let him go if you put my brother in front of me."

"Diego couldn't have gotten here so fast," Xav said in a reasonable tone. "It has to be someone else messing with you. Maybe those guys from California want their money back."

By Dean's tightening grip on Xav's arm, he saw the logic in

this point. He jerked Xav directly in front of him. "You're going in first and flushing them out."

"You mean the two of us against whoever managed to break in here and take out all your guys?" Xav asked incredulously. "Good plan. How about we get the hell out of here and drive to the rendezvous, instead?"

"What about your girlfriend?" Dean sounded surprised. "You'd just leave her? You're cold, dude."

"They've probably already nabbed her." Xav shrugged as though ready to cut his losses. "Linds," he called. "You all right? Answer if you can."

There was a long moment of silence. Just when Xav thought Lindsay wouldn't respond, they heard her voice from the depths of the darkness. It was weak, pleading.

"Xav, honey? They say to stay back."

Xav tried not to sag in relief. Lindsay Cummings would never, ever cry out to anyone so pathetically, no matter what the situation. If someone truly held her, she'd be either snarling obscenities or teasing her captors into confusion, as she had with Dean and his henchmen in the office.

"Okay, you're right, they have her," Dean said quietly. "We're going."

"You'd just leave all your guys?" Xav asked, mimicking Dean's earlier question. "That's cold, dude."

"If they could help, they already would have. Let's go."

Dean turned Xav around and half pushed, half dragged him toward the locked outer door. Xav heard a faint scratching sound behind them, maybe claws across a floor, then the squeal that sounded like a door that hadn't been opened in a while, followed by a slight draft that quickly cut off.

Dean whirled, pointing his gun into the darkness. Xav readied himself to disarm him, but Dean almost immediately turned back and continued shoving Xav at the door. At some point, Dean would have to undo the padlock or reach for a key to have Xav unlock it, and Xav would seize his chance.

Something clicked above them, and then static buzzed through whatever speakers had once been this place's intercom system.

"Oh, wow," Lindsay's voice came to them. "This is like the control room for the whole warehouse, isn't it?"

"Where is this control room?" Xav demanded instantly of Dean. "Come on. We can still help her."

"Nope, she's screwed." Dean continued propelling Xav onward. "So are we, if we stay. I have other resources. You just make sure I get my meetup with AC."

"Lindsay." Xav tried once again to sound like the concerned but resigned boyfriend. "I'm sorry."

Something gurgled deep in the recesses of the building. Dean halted, his gun solidly on Xav, his gaze darting everywhere. Xav braced himself for whatever Lindsay was about to do.

The broken pipes above them began to shudder and groan.

With a loud *bang,* water burst from them, cascading in haphazard fountains and raining down to shelves, crates, and the cement floor. The sudden pressure found weak joints in other pipes, and soon more jets of water spurted forth, spraying Dean and Xav in an abrupt shower of cold water.

"I think I found the sprinkler system," Lindsay said through the speakers. "Hope that stuff is potable."

Gee, thanks, Xav said silently.

"What does this do?" Lindsay went on. "Oh, it opens the loading docks. Cool."

With a creak and a squeal, the three large garage doors near the exit Dean had been making for slowly rose and folded back to reveal the cold darkness outside.

Dean swiped at the water running down his face. "What the hell?" he snarled.

"Forgot to mention, Lindsay's a little crazy," Xav said smugly.

"Let's go." In his single-minded need to confront his brother, Dean started pushing Xav toward the rising doors.

Chill air rushed into the warehouse. While Xav saw only darkness in their immediate area, the glow in the sky beyond came unmistakably from Las Vegas. The occasional flash from light shows on the Strip confirmed it.

The two men were steps away from rushing through an open garage door when it gave an alarming creak. Xav propelled himself and Dean backward as all three doors shot downward, slamming to the floor with a reverberating crash.

"No, you don't," Lindsay said above them. "You okay, Xav?"

"Barely." Xav struggled with Dean who, instead of scrambling clear when Xav pushed him, had locked an arm around Xav's neck.

Xav went still when he felt the barrel of Dean's pistol in his ribs.

At the same time, someone hammered on the outside doors. "Parkes. You all right in there?"

"I guess there really are more guards outside," Lindsay proclaimed through the speakers. "Let's see, shall we?"

Intense light flared beyond the high windows, and shouts came to them.

"My, those floodlights are *bright*," Lindsay said cheerily. "Take your hands off my mate, Mr. Dean Parkes, or I won't go easy on you."

"I have a pistol against your *mate*, as you call him," Dean announced. "Come out of there."

"You really shouldn't count on weapons, you know," Lindsay said without concern. "So unreliable."

"That's it," Dean snarled. "I'm done."

Xav jerked sideways, jabbing his elbow into Dean at the same time. He broke Dean's hold, but before he could dive out of the way, Dean fired his pistol straight into Xav's stomach.

Or would have, if the gun had gone off. Instead, it clicked. When Dean glanced at the weapon in surprise, Xav tackled him.

"Nice one," Lindsay called. "That's why I lifted your gun and emptied it before I went shopping."

"Son of a bitch," Dean snarled as he fought.

"By the way," Lindsay went on, her words growing vibrant. "Xavier Escobar, under the light of the moon, the Mother Goddess, and before witnesses, I accept your mate-claim!"

"*Shit.*" Xav gasped.

He took Dean's blows and returned his own, the two men fighting with swift violence. Xav finally broke from Dean, rolling away from the man across the smooth floor. Dean scrambled to his feet and started to run.

"I love you, Linds!" Xav yelled into the air as he sprang up and charged after Dean. "Shouldn't there be more witnesses, though? Better ones than this dickhead?"

"Oh, there are plenty of *witnesses*." Lindsay's laughter rang out, the most beautiful sound Xav knew. That is, next to her groaning his name when he was buried deep inside her.

The dock's doors rolled upward once more. The guards Dean had prudently stationed outside the building were now lying on the concrete loading bays in motionless lumps.

Dean pelted out, regardless, Xav right behind him.

"AC," Dean screamed when he saw his brother illuminated by the floodlights. "I'll kill you—"

AC, held between a pissed-off wolf Shifter with a giant

sword and a massive man with orange-and-black striped hair, lunged forward. "No, little brother, I'm killing *you*."

An instant later, Xav tackled Dean once more. Blood dripped from Xav's face onto Dean's as Dean struggled and spit obscenities.

A pair of familiar combat boots halted near Xav, then Diego calmly bent down and wrapped Dean's wrists in zip ties. Diego stepped back to allow a thin but surprisingly muscular man with dark hair and midnight eyes haul Dean to his feet.

Xav rolled quickly out of the way. If Stuart Reid started teleporting people, Xav didn't want to be caught in the field of weirdness.

He climbed to his feet to find Lindsay right in front of him, her green eyes wide with both concern and elation.

She was stark naked, meaning she'd left her clothes behind when she'd shifted, but she showed no uneasiness about the other Shifters and humans surrounding her. She latched onto Xav and pulled him close, holding him shakily.

"Did you mean it?" she whispered.

"Which part?" Xav breathed into her ear. "That I love you? Or that we needed better witnesses? I admit, these are pretty good ones."

In addition to Diego, Neal, Tiger, and Reid, Cassidy was there, along with Leah, who watched the two of them, enraptured, tears on her face.

"The first part." Lindsay touched her forehead to Xav's. "I love you too, Xav." Her voice was quiet, pitched only so Xav would hear.

Xav's body heated, something inside him complete for the first time in his life.

"You meant it about the mate-claim?" Xav asked. "You weren't just trying to distract Dean?"

"Couldn't it be both?" Lindsay smiled at him. "But, in case

we didn't make it, I wanted to be your mate when I went to the Summerland. I want that even *more* if we're staying right here on Earth. Mate bond or no mate bond, I don't care."

"Linds." Xav cupped her face and kissed her, a slow, hot, promising kiss. She sank into him, her returning kiss full of sultry fire.

Small claws on his back jerked Xav from the bliss of Lindsay. One of the wolf cubs—Matt or Kyle—scrambled up onto Xav's shoulder and began a high-pitched, ear-splitting howl.

Xav put a hand on the little guy's furry back. "I love you too, *lobito.*"

"He's congratulating you on the mate bond," Neal translated. "I am too."

Lindsay's eyes were starry with hope. "I feel it." She laid her hand on Xav's chest, right over his heart. "I think you might too. Do you?"

The hot tingle inside Xav flared at her touch. It quickly became searing need that made him wish everyone else would evaporate while he took Lindsay on this cold loading bay floor.

"I think so." Xav slid his hands to her hips. "I don't really understand it, but I'm willing to let you teach me all about it."

"That sounds fun." Lindsay's answer was shy but her touch promised wonderful things to come.

"The mate bond is there." Tiger's resonant voice came to them. He sounded as though it should be obvious. "It is easy to see."

Matt, or Kyle, on Xav's shoulder, howled his agreement, while his twin dashed around their feet, yipping.

Lindsay ignored them all and tugged Xav to her for another kiss, this one filled with deep desire. Xav felt himself reacting, his body not caring that they stood in the middle of a crowd.

He remembered his talk with Lindsay about scent marking, mating, and the mate bond, and knew the mate bond was important to her—one of the most important things in a Shifter's life. Lindsay had just tossed out that she didn't care whether it formed, but Xav knew she did.

The burning in his chest told Xav Tiger was right. Somehow, the mate bond had found him, and now was making him want Lindsay with an intensity he couldn't fight.

Talking and bonding could come later. For now, Xav needed Lindsay, the mate of his heart. The kiss turned even more fervent.

Behind them Brody guffawed. "Get a room."

Lindsay broke from Xav with a laugh, but her eyes held the same burning need Xav felt. Xav cupped her face.

"I feel it," he assured Lindsay. The hope in Lindsay's eyes seared him, and he traced her silken cheek. "Mate of my heart."

Amid the continuing laughter and Emma's admonishing *Leave them alone, Bear,* Xav gathered Lindsay close and kissed her again.

The two who'd danced around each other, in and out, back and forth, with the occasional connection were now whole. One.

Mates.

CHAPTER TWENTY-ONE

I t took far longer to get out the warehouse than Xav liked.

He wanted to stay buried in his kiss with Lindsay and then run out of there with her to his place—or maybe to the back of an SUV on the side of the road if they couldn't make it that far—but Shifters surged around them, full of congratulations or more teasing.

When Xav and Lindsay finally broke apart, Cassidy stepped behind Lindsay and draped the shirt and pants Lindsay must have shed to shift over her shoulders. "You'll need these," she said in amusement. "At least until you get to Xav's."

Lindsay flushed as she caught the clothes and slid them on in swift movements. "Thanks, Cass. Always looking out for me."

Once she was dressed, Lindsay turned and opened her arms for her mother. Leah gathered her in, Martin joining them, the three sharing a silent, tight embrace.

They didn't need to speak, Xav realized. They'd been through so much together that they could convey their love and relief without words.

When they finally parted, Lindsay wiped her eyes. Leah didn't bother, tears trickling unashamedly down her cheeks. The usually quiet Martin beamed, his face wet.

"I found the cutest stuff in there." Lindsay gestured to the warehouse as she drew a shaky breath. "Sweet T-shirts and the most adorable shoes. Think anyone would mind if we took them? Who do they belong to?"

Of course, Lindsay wouldn't let anything like life-and-death situations or accepting a mate-claim keep her from shopping.

"No one," Neal told her. "This warehouse was abandoned by a start-up and foreclosed on, and the goods inside are scheduled to be destroyed, if anyone can be bothered. Your buddy Dean was negotiating to buy it through a shell company."

So he wouldn't be reported as a squatter, Xav mused. Dean might run an illegal business out it, but he couldn't be arrested for simply hanging out on his own property.

"Cool." Lindsay said, her usual verve returning. She paused to kiss Xav again, tearing herself from him before it could heat up. "Coming, ladies? We won't be long," she confided to Xav and Diego.

With another promising smile at Xav, Lindsay laced her arms through Cassidy's and her mother's and drew them back into the building.

"Sure, they won't." Diego heaved a resigned sigh. "Well, it gives us time to get all these guys trussed up and into our vans. You all right, Xav?"

"Yeah," Xav said in surprise. "I feel great." He'd been tranqued, hauled for miles to a cold warehouse, kept under threat without food or water, and threatened with his life. And yet, he knew he could run a marathon, or at least a half, or do more skiing up on the mountain, without any trouble at all.

"Touch of a mate," Tiger rumbled.

"Agreed," Diego said with a nod. "The touch of a true mate can heal a lot of hurting. Welcome to the club, bro."

Then Diego, his straitlaced, by-the-rules older brother, swiftly caught Xav in a hard hug.

"Thanks for coming to my rescue." Xav thumped Diego on the back as they eased apart. "One more time."

"Always." The warmth in Diego's eyes told Xav all he needed to know.

Diego had been watching out for Xav since Xav could remember, not because of obligation, Xav had realized as they'd grown older, but out of love. Diego could have decided not to bother with Xav at all, but he'd done everything in his power to make sure his troublesome little brother made it into the light and had a good life.

It beat the hell out of the toxic relationship of AC and Dean.

When Diego turned away to help his men and the Shifters shove Dean, AC, and his unconscious thugs into the waiting SUVs, Leah slipped from inside the warehouse to catch Xav in an embrace. She held on tight, her residual tears wetting Xav's shirt.

"I'm so happy for you both," she said tremulously. "Lindsay needs you, Xavier. She's always so much stronger when she's with you."

Lindsay was plenty strong on her own, but Xav understood. "I'm stronger with *her*."

Two halves. Make them whole.

Tiger's words rang in Xav's head. Well, Xav intended to do just that, in all ways.

"The mate bond knows," Leah said with confidence. "Martin will be glad for a reason to finish that suite he's been building in the basement. It will be perfect for you and Lindsay, and of course, cubs."

She turned away before Xav could open his mouth to say

a word, hurrying back inside to be with her daughter, whose laughter poured out to him.

"I *have* a house," Xav said to no one.

It stood to reason, though, that Xav would move in with Lindsay. She couldn't legally live outside of Shiftertown, nor would she want to be far from her family.

Xav found, upon consideration, that he didn't mind. He was already close to his in-laws-to-be, and it felt weird to live too much apart from Diego anyway. Now Xav and Diego would be backdoor neighbors.

He could hang onto the house he'd worked so hard to buy, and either rent it out, or use it for private getaways for himself and Lindsay. Shifters liked to be in everybody's business.

But ... "Cubs?" Was it too soon to be thinking about having them?

"Lindsay is already carrying one," Tiger informed him as he lumbered by.

"What?" Xav stared at him, but Tiger continued into the warehouse without pausing. Xav hurried after him. "Tiger, what did you say?"

Tiger lifted an inert man over his shoulder with ease. "I said Lindsay is already carrying a cub." He pointed to his own golden eyes. "I can see."

"Crap. How do you ...?" Xav broke off. Tiger had unusual abilities that no one, even Tiger, understood. "Are you sure?"

Tiger gave him a grave nod. "I'm always sure." He walked away from Xav and out to deposit his load in the SUV.

Vehicles began to start up. "Xav!" Diego's shout came.

It meant he was ready to go and not wanting to wait. Like Lindsay and her parents, Xav and Diego didn't always need a lot of words to understand each other.

"Linds," Xav called into the recesses of the warehouse. "We're going."

Did she answer right away? Pull Cassidy and her mom out with her to hurry to their mates?

Nope. Xav paced while he waited, and Diego leaned on the horn.

At long last, Cassidy and Lindsay strolled out from one of the aisles, arms full of clothing, shoes hanging from fingers. Leah followed with a more modest bundle, which she carried past Xav and out of the building.

Lindsay dropped half the shoes she carried. "We should grab one of these empty crates," she suggested.

"Good idea." Cassidy made for one. She and Lindsay piled their stuff inside, then they both looked hopefully at Xav.

"You are kidding me," Xav said. He should be annoyed they wanted to use him as a pack animal, but the merriment on Lindsay's face made him want to laugh.

Thinking about what Tiger had just told him sent Xav to the crate. He peered inside at the folded shirts, skirts, and dresses, and small pairs of shoes arranged in neat rows. The shoes were for children, not full-grown Shifter adults.

"You'll never fit into those," Xav joked. "I remember you agreeing to AC's job because you said you needed more shoes. And asked Dean to let you go hunting for them."

"I did." Lindsay's eyes sparkled as she pushed her hair from her face. "I didn't say the shoes were for *me*."

Cassidy grinned at Xav. "They're for Jinx's cubs."

"All the littler ones are still growing," Lindsay said. "They go through shoes like you wouldn't believe."

Xav gaped at her until he realized he was, and snapped his mouth shut. Lindsay was confirming what Xav had known all along—that she could act frivolous and empty-headed, but she did so to hide a kind heart and keen understanding.

Xav would have to show her she didn't have to hide anymore.

Lindsay nodded at the crate. "Ready to go. Though ... wait a sec, Cass. There was that blue satin sheath you were debating about—"

"*No.*" Xav cut her off. He hefted the crate in his arms, trying not to stagger under its weight. "Let's roll, before Diego wears out that horn."

Cassidy laughed. "You'd think living with Shifters would teach him patience. Coming, love." She hurried out the door, waving at Diego as she went.

"Let me help you with that." Lindsay caught a sagging side of the crate, balancing it between them. "The two of us can do anything together. Right?"

Xav lifted the crate out of her grasp. "You keep saving *my* ass," he said. "Now, let me save yours."

"I'm plenty capable of balancing a *box*, Escobar," Lindsay said hotly. "You should have seen me leaping around those shelves."

Xav grimaced. "I'm glad I didn't. Especially after what Tiger told me."

"What did he tell you?" Lindsay asked in sudden curiosity. "Tiger's always full of surprises."

"He said we're having a cub." Xav began carrying the crate to the outer doors. "Who will apparently live with us in your parent's basement."

He heard Lindsay's sharp intake of breath and then the quick pattering of her bare feet to catch up with him. "Are you serious?"

"Yep," Xav said without stopping. "I bet Leah is talking to Martin about the construction details even now."

"No, you aggravating male. About the cub."

Xav halted and set down the crate to face her. Diego could wait a minute. "Tiger seems to think it's true."

Lindsay's eyes were wide. "Carly says he always knows. Shit, Xav. A cub. That's wonderful. And terrifying."

Xav stepped to her. "Like you said, we can do anything together."

Lindsay regarded him in almost pure fear. "Can we?"

"Yes." Xav's uncertainty fled as love for this untamed and beautiful woman surged through him. He cupped her shoulders and pulled her close. "We can. The mate bond knows so."

Lindsay leaned into him, her warmth like an embrace. "Our cub will be awesome."

"And a serious handful. But we can do this."

Lindsay's smile trembled. "Yeah. We can. Try and let anyone stop us."

Xav grinned at her. "They can try."

"But they never will." Lindsay pulled him down to her for a brief, hot kiss.

Xav gathered her in before she could let go, what he now knew was the mate bond flowing through them. With it came the mating frenzy that had been building in him for some time, the need to constantly be with his mate, their bodies entwined, no matter what.

The rapid beating of a horn outside was accompanied by two wolf cubs racing around them, yipping at the tops of their voices.

Lindsay and Xav broke apart, laughing, but the yearning hadn't receded.

Xav took Lindsay by the hand and led his mate out after the careening cubs to the waiting Shifters and his loving family.

CHAPTER TWENTY-TWO

The mating ceremony, held that weekend, was blessed with a warm day and a cool and clear night. Eric performed the sun ceremony in the afternoon, which initiated the link between mated Shifters.

Lindsay fought her mating frenzy as she stood next to Xav in the little grove of olive trees, because if she didn't, she'd seize him and run away with him to his house, where they could lose themselves in each other. She'd never want to leave his bed for days, and by Xav's hot glances at her, he wouldn't either.

But then, they'd miss the full moon for the ceremony tonight and have to wait nearly another month for it. The moon ceremony was the most important one, and so Lindsay repressed her burning needs.

As she politely listened to Eric, a crown of flowers in her hair, she pressed her hand to her abdomen, thinking she could already feel the flutter of the cub inside.

Xav's cub. He or she would have Xav's warm smile and dark eyes, she was certain of it. And it would turn into a pure lynx with mischievous tendencies.

Lindsay was torn between elation and terror about their coming cub. She consoled herself by recalling that her mom and dad, who'd had so much experience with her, would live upstairs. With them, plus Cassidy and Diego nearby, she couldn't lose.

Xav, who had a kind and caring heart behind his fun-loving facade, would be a great dad. Lindsay knew this without doubt.

She'd told Xav how she'd done a sort-of striptease for Dean's guard in the warehouse so she could disrobe to shift without rousing his suspicions. Instead of being enraged, as a possessive male might be, Xav had laughed soundly and praised her inventiveness.

His understanding of her floored her, and then spiked Lindsay's ever-present mating need. They'd had to spend a long time alone in his house working that off.

Once Eric finally pronounced the mate blessing, and Shifters began to party, complete with afternoon cookout, Lindsay made herself, after one burning kiss with Xav, stay apart from him the rest of the day.

She busied herself helping Cassidy prepare for the huge celebration that would follow the Moon ceremony, keeping her crown of flowers fresh in Cassidy's refrigerator.

Lindsay and Cassidy had taken Jinx's cubs the sneakers they'd liberated from the warehouse a few days ago, and now the little ones sprinted around in them, showing them off to anyone who would look.

While they worked in Cassidy's kitchen, Lindsay again scolded her friend for risking herself coming to the rescue, but Cassidy only regarded her stubbornly.

"Me staying behind wasn't going to happen," Cassidy said as she chopped cold potatoes for the salad she was putting together. "I knew you'd need me, and your mom did too." She drew a breath. "In case anything happened to Xav."

Lindsay's heart chilled, and she tore apart a batch of cilantro in her agitation, its fragrance filling the room.

Cassidy meant that if Lindsay had lost Xav that night, the mate bond would have been severed, and Lindsay's grief would have known no end. A broken mate bond left the survivor devastated, which Cassidy well knew.

"This is why you're my best friend," Lindsay said, dropping the cilantro leaves to wrap an arm around Cassidy's shoulder. Cassidy touched her golden head to Lindsay's, neither of them needing to say more.

"How did you all track us, anyway?" Lindsay asked briskly as she tossed Cassidy's chopped potatoes with oil and the now-shredded herb. "I never heard that part of the story. Been busy." Her face heated, because Cassidy knew exactly what had absorbed her these past few days.

"Your mom showed us your text," she said. "Neal traced the number via the Guardian Network to a guy who used to be in AC's gang. Diego then talked to Jeff, who revealed that the man was now in Dean's gang, and that Dean was its leader. Jeff knew just enough about where the new hideout *might* be to point us in that direction, though he hadn't been there yet. We followed his route to the far west side of town and drove around until Tiger picked up your scent and directed us to the abandoned warehouse. Simple."

"Simple. Right." Lindsay flashed Cassidy a skeptical look. "I can't tell you how happy I was to see you all pull up. Though I had everything covered. I was going to finish taking out the guards and Dean and then grab Xav and run off. But I appreciate the effort." She shrugged. "And the ride home."

"You shit." Cassidy came to Lindsay, returning her earlier hug. Lindsay laid down her spoon and enjoyed the close moment. "I'm so happy for you, Linds," Cassidy whispered. "You deserve this."

"I do, don't I?" Lindsay blinked back tears as they parted.

"And hey, we got some great new clothes out of it. Best kidnapping ever."

Cassidy laughed and they both returned to the feast preparations, Lindsay basking in the knowledge of how lucky she was to have so many people who truly loved her.

———

"YOU READY FOR THIS?" XAV ASKED SOFTLY.

He stood beside Lindsay as the Shifters swayed into the circle dance—Shifters moving in concentric circles around Xav and Lindsay, family and close friends in the nearest one.

Lindsay was so happy, it almost frightened her. She gripped Xav's hand. "I couldn't run even if I wanted to. We're surrounded."

Xav smiled, the warmest and best sight in Lindsay's life. "I like this custom."

Petals from the floral crown tickled her cheek as she grinned in return. "So do I, actually. Hey, isn't that Jeff?" She nodded at a man awkwardly standing with a set of crutches in the outer circle, watching the Shifters around him, including Graham, who kept a stern eye on him.

"Diego brought him. Jeff says he worked for Dean only because he desperately needed the money for his kids, and since he helped us and Diego didn't actually witness him commit any crimes, we didn't turn him over to the police with the rest of them. Maybe Jeff will learn his lesson and go straight, live a blameless life."

"That would be nice," Lindsay said. "Graham is busy intimidating him."

"He wouldn't be Graham if he didn't. Diego's going to find something for Jeff to do for us. Like he did with Emma."

"Sounds great," Lindsay said truthfully. She felt sorry for Jeff, who'd been hurt and left for dead by people he trusted.

Plus, his intel had helped ensure that Xav returned home safely, for which Lindsay would be eternally grateful.

She was also pleased that no jealous dart laced her anymore at the mention of Emma's name. Lindsay had the feeling she and Emma were going to be great friends.

Emma was there today, her sunny nature letting her banter with the Shifters without worry. Even Graham's Lupines gave her grudging respect. Only Brody was prickly with her, and she with him. Lindsay smiled to herself. Something going on there, definitely.

"By the way," Xav said. "Did you rub it in Graham's face that you chose a mate? I did."

Lindsay nodded. "I did mention it several dozen times, but Graham truly is happy for us. As well as relieved he doesn't have to deal with his Lupines about me anymore."

"He can move on to everything else on his plate," Xav said with sympathy. "Uh oh." He jerked his chin at Leah and Juanita, who were marginally following the dance steps in the inner circle, the taller Shifter woman bending down to say something to Xav's minute mother. "My mom and yours are conspiring. That doesn't bode well."

Lindsay edged closer to him. "Makes me glad you kept your house."

"Which they both know how to get to," Xav reminded her.

They shared a trepidatious look. "We'll deal with that when we have to," Lindsay whispered.

Before Xav could answer, Eric approached, the usually laid-back man smiling broadly.

"Ready, you two?"

Lindsay turned to Xav, her mate, her other self, the man she'd loved since the moment she'd first seen him. Her Shifter cat had known it, even if Lindsay's human side had taken a long time to catch up.

Her lynx let out a purr. "You bet I am," she told Eric.

Xav gave Eric a decided nod. "Let's do this."

Eric beckoned to Iona, who left Cassidy's side to join her mate. Both faced Xav and Lindsay, Iona's face alight with gladness.

Eric put his large hands on Xav's and Lindsay's clasped ones. Iona's joined his, and Eric raised their collective hands high. "Under the light of the full moon, the Mother Goddess, I proclaim you mates!"

A riotous cheer followed. Music blared and the sedate circle dance segued into a wild frenzy, clothes tearing as animals threw them off and began to howl and roar.

"I love you, Xav," Lindsay yelled at him over the noise.

"I love you, Lindsay. My *mate*."

Xav lifted her against him and spun around with her, then took her mouth in a scorching kiss. The shouting and joyful screaming faded as Lindsay became absorbed in Xav, embracing the savage happiness inside her.

"Maybe we should sneak off to our house now," Xav said into her ear when the kiss ended.

Lindsay could only nod, her mating frenzy ramping so high it robbed her of speech.

Xav grabbed her hand, and together they fled through the celebrating Shifters, who didn't bother to impede their escape.

A gust of wind tore the crown from Lindsay's head and sent it into the night. Moonlight caught on the chain of flowers, symbols of her unwavering love for Xav and the powerful strength of the mate bond.

ALSO BY JENNIFER ASHLEY

Shifters Unbound

Pride Mates

Primal Bonds

Bodyguard

Wild Cat

Hard Mated

Mate Claimed

"Perfect Mate" (novella)

Lone Wolf

Tiger Magic

Feral Heat

Wild Wolf

Bear Attraction

Mate Bond

Lion Eyes

Bad Wolf

Wild Things

White Tiger

Guardian's Mate

Red Wolf

Midnight Wolf

Tiger Striped

A Shifter Christmas Carol

Iron Master

The Last Warrior

Tiger's Daughter

Bear Facts

Stray Cat

Shifter Made ("Prequel" novella)

Stormwalker Series (w/a Allyson James)

Stormwalker

Firewalker

Shadow Walker

"Double Hexed"

Nightwalker

Dreamwalker

Dragon Bites

Wing Dancer

Shape Changer

SHIFTERS UNBOUND SERIES BY SHIFTERTOWN

Austin Shifters
Pride Mates (Liam and Kim)
Primal Bonds (Sean and Andrea)
Bodyguard (Ronan and Elizabeth)
Hard Mated (Spike and Myka)
Lone Wolf (Ellison and Maria)
Tiger Magic (Tiger and Carly:
Tiger first appears in *Mate Claimed*, Las Vegas Shifters)
Feral Heat (Deni and Jace.
Jace crosses over from the Las Vegas Shifters)
Bear Attraction (Walker and Rebecca.
Crosses over to Kendrick's group)
Bad Wolf (Broderick and Joanne.
Briefly crosses with Montana Shiftertown)
Wild Things (Mason and Jasmine.
Intro of haunted house and Zander)
Tiger Striped (Tiger and Carly novella)
A Shifter Christmas Carol
(novella featuring Dylan)

The Last Warrior (Ben and Rhianne)
(Ben crosses over to other Shiftertowns)
Tiger's Daughter (Connor and Tiger-Girl)

Kendrick's Group
(Most cross over with Austin Shifters)
Lion Eyes (Seamus and Bree)
White Tiger (Kendrick and Addison)
Red Wolf (Jaycee and Dimitri)

Las Vegas Shifters
Wild Cat (Cassidy and Diego)
Mate Claimed (Eric and Iona)
Perfect Mate (Nell and Cormac)
Wild Wolf (Graham and Misty)
Iron Master (Stuart Reid and Peigi)
Bear Facts (Shane and Freya)
Stray Cat (Xav and Lindsay)

North Carolina Shifters
Mate Bond (Bowman and Kenzie.
Crossover with Las Vegas Shifters)

New Orleans Shifters
Midnight Wolf (Angus and Tamsin.
Crosses over with Austin Shifters and Zander)

Montana Shifters
Guardian's Mate (Zander and Rae)

Note: I include Zander with the Montana Shifters, because
Rae is from the Montana Shiftertown, but Zander moves
between all the groups. It's his way.

Check my website:

    https://www.jenniferashley.com

    for additions as I continue to explore all the Shiftertowns!

    All my best,

    Jennifer Ashley

ABOUT THE AUTHOR

New York Times bestselling and award-winning author Jennifer Ashley has more than 100 published novels and novellas in mystery, romance, historical fiction, and urban fantasy under the names Jennifer Ashley, Allyson James, and Ashley Gardner. Jennifer's books have been translated into more than a dozen languages and have earned starred reviews in *Publisher's Weekly* and *Booklist*. When she isn't writing, Jennifer enjoys playing music (guitar, piano, flute), reading, hiking, cooking, and building dollhouse miniatures.

More about Jennifer's books can be found at
http://www.jenniferashley.com

To keep up to date on her new releases, join her newsletter here:
http://eepurl.com/47kLL